Rapid Transits

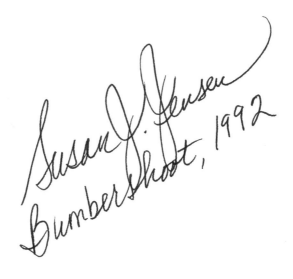
Susan J. Jensen
Bumbershoot, 1992

Rapid Transits

and Other Stories

Holley Rubinsky

POLESTAR
BOOK PUBLISHERS

Published by
Polestar Press Ltd., R.R. 1, Winlaw, B.C. VOG 2J0
604 226 7670

Distributed by
Raincoast Book Distribution Ltd., 112 East 3rd Avenue,
Vancouver, B.C., V5T 1C8
604 873 6581

Published with the assistance of the Canada Council.
Some of the stories in this collection have been published previously
as follows: "Rapid Transits" in *The Malahat Review* and *The Journey
Prize Anthology* (McClelland & Stewart Inc., 1989); "Grounding"
and "Flight" in *The Malahat Review;* "Coast Highway" in *Rubicon;*
"Capricorn Women" in *Canadian Fiction Magazine;* "Preacher's
Geese" in *The Malahat Review* and *The Macmillan Anthology I*
(Macmillan of Canada, 1988); earlier versions of "On an Island" and
"Embers" in *Event.* I am deeply grateful to the Ontario Arts
Council and the Canada Council for timely financial assistance.
Thanks also to Debra, Fern, Jeannie, Bobbi and Peter, Robin and
my mother; Donna Bennett, David Jackson, Alistair MacLeod, Joe
Rogers, Constance Rooke, Leon Rooke, Julian Ross, Dale Zieroth
for the talks by the Bow, and Yuri.

Cover by Jim Brennan
Text Design by Nelson Adams
Produced by Polestar in Winlaw, B.C.
Printed and bound in Canada

Canadian Cataloguing in Publication Data
Rubinsky, Holley, 1943-
Rapid transits and other stories
ISBN 0-919591-56-6
I. Title.

PS8585.U24R3 1990   C813'.54   C90-091585-4
PR9199.3.R82R3 1990

Contents

I

Harriet Mary Dawn

Rapid Transits   9
Grounding   21
Flight   40

II

Lost and Found

Coast Highway   81
Capricorn Women   95
Preacher's Geese   110
On an Island   120
Embers   134
My Daghter   142

III

California

Breakdowns of Any Kind   157
The Next Governor of California   175

I

Harriet Mary Dawn

Rapid Transits

My da isn't that old, but he has a tremor of the hands that shivers up to his neck and gives his head a quick snap once in a while. So small a movement that you'd hardly notice, but I've been watching him my whole life. "I thought it would of come, Harriet," he says of the baby and my belly sticking half way out to here, but I can only shrug. Some creatures have more sense than others; they stay where the staying's good.

"Fine hotel, maybe," I say, but he doesn't get it and frowns. His eyebrows are so sparse and light, you can hardly see them. "Good room," I say, tapping my belly. "Pool and all. Cheap."

He grins then and shows his missing front tooth that used to scare me. All a man needs is to let a little stubble grow and have a front tooth missing and it doesn't matter who he is, he looks bad. One day the tooth was just gone, fell out over meatloaf in a cafeteria downtown he said. It took my mother some doing to make him wear a false one, and then he took to flicking it when you least expected it.

I have him in the kitchen, sitting on a straight-back chair, facing me. I know he's not comfortable, you can see how his elbows on the table are holding up his weight, but Bill doesn't have much furniture, he never needed it. "Did you like the bus?"

"I dislike buses," he says, sounding grand like something he's rehearsed in front of a mirror. "I am so used now to travelling by air." Anybody can see from his shiny suit and thin cheeks that this fellow couldn't afford a plane from one side of Timbuktu (the one in California) to the other, but it doesn't stop him lying. He needs to do it.

I offer him an apple, but he shakes his head sadly. He tilts his chin back and opens up and I see he hasn't got much left, maybe enough for chomping Gerbers Junior dinners. He shrugs, though, and looks at me and smiles. When he smiles, his eyes water as though he might cry. Eyes like my da's, ripe and juicy, slightly past prime like good stewing fruit, usually mean a person doesn't have a grip on things. Once he said to my auntie: How does a baby come out such a small hole?

My da has come all this way to see his grandbaby, but there is none, yet.

Before I spied him down the road at the bottom of the hill and my heart started to sink, I was sitting happy and round as a pumpkin under an apple tree. The apples are Gravensteins and Bill says they're having an on-year; they're big and tart and crispy. Foam was gathering at the corners of my mouth as I chewed. I have big horse-like teeth, but it doesn't bother me. When you're born funny-looking or have a speech defect or epilepsy, after a while you realize you don't have too much to worry about, because the worst has already happened. I don't know whether I read this somewhere or made it up.

It's my fault he's here. The time not to write a letter to someone you haven't seen in a blue moon is when you're suddenly feeling a little lonely for them and sorry for them, both feelings together. Having found this little town and a job in the hardware store where I met Bill, maybe in the dither of my own good fortune, I wrote my da at his last address, a boarding house in Eureka CA.

"So you're settled down," he says, wracking his brain for conversation. When you're as pregnant as I am, you don't mind just sitting and seeing what happens next.

"You might say."

"Is this feller the father?"

I'd laugh if it wasn't so sad. I have to turn my face away quick. I've been telling people it's a lover who died of leukemia. That kind of thing.

He's staring at my tits that have got even bigger. "Wisht it was mine," he says and that opens a whole new kettle of fish.

In my teens, I expected a dwarf would rape me. It was the worst thing I could think of, I was young then, and all the other girls wanted to date the tall, good-looking fellows on the basketball or football teams, but I didn't stand a chance. Even if I were to take off my clothes and fall into a helpless swoon, they would've just laughed, because my body isn't an attractive one. It doesn't have smooth tits with rosebud tips or a slender wasp-like waist or curved hips. My hips are up too high, like somebody who has fallen from a tall building and landed feet first, what would happen then. Your heels would push leg bones which would push the hip bones, which would tuck up too near the bottom of the rib cage. In this way, except for being normal height, I look a bit like a dwarf myself, that squat, solid sort of hunched look, like you couldn't knock them over with a feather and better not try.

I have the kind of tits that never were young. Not creamy or perky, certainly no tidy handful. When they started to grow I was eleven and built chunky and they just took off. While other girls were whining about training bras I was wrapping gauze tightly around my chest, which just made me look even more barrel-chested. The tits came in veined and droopy, full and big. They looked like those of a full-grown woman who had given birth to seven babies and nursed them all. I didn't think they were exactly ugly, there was something remarkable about them, I saw kinds like mine on fertility goddesses in books, for example, but other people did. Think them ugly. But I suspect too much of a good thing just scared the shit out of them.

I offer him more coffee. He nods yes, yes and then I go ahead and put out some shortbreads I made just yesterday. He drops crumbs when he eats because his tongue does a lot of work, mashing the bits on the roof of his mouth. He's hungry, though, and like any woman, I begin cataloguing what's in the fridge, and imagine dishes: spaghetti, piping hot with tons of Parmesan on top, or the corn-and-hamburger casserole flavored with chili that Bill likes. Seeing my da is like being in a dream; it was my dreaming brought him here, to this unlikely place.

In one dream, I'm looking down at him while he is thumping me on the head like he used to do, for fun I guess; he said his da did that to him and I should know what it felt like. That time, I was outside playing in the dirt with some captured caterpillars (the black furry kind, their insides the brightest yellow and green), when he came along and raised me up by my arm until I was standing, and then he put his hand under my little green and white checkered dress and pinched my tummy and then he started thumping me on the head, with his thumb and middle finger, like you do tiddlywinks, still holding me and saying something, I don't recall what. He smelled like what later I knew was Old Spice and whiskey. His nose was red, he was starting to cry. Meanwhile, thump thump on the crown of my head and me writhing and wiggling and squirming. Just then a swallowtail butterfly fluttered through the garden and in my mind I ran after its red-with-the-black-dot targeted tail until I caught up and then I fluttered away, and my da was left thumping on an abandoned body, though the bruise on my arm lasted.

Probably he didn't thump me often. I remember it, but that's kids, if they have a certain turn of mind, they remember all the bad things. I was proud, like most kids are. Mess with them once, they never forget.

Just then the outside door swings open, the latches make rattly sounds, and Bill comes onto the service porch that's just off the kitchen, thumps mud off his boots. He's been over the way working gardens all day. When he stamps his feet, the whole kitchen shakes a bit, because the house is wood, and old, and has a very comforting smell of wood stove, grease, and rust. Bill has tools he's collected from other old-timers slung on great big nails. My da wipes his face on his sleeve, reminding me I have forgot to put out napkins, and then brushes his lips with his smooth fingers to be extra sure. I see by this behavior that he wants to impress Bill. I see by the way he squares back his shoulders and sets his face kind of proud yet humble that he wants something. I also see he's going to be mighty surprised, as Bill puts it. When Bill opens the door to the kitchen, I stay sat for the introductions. It's part of getting away with a lot when you're pregnant. My da's transparent eyebrows raise up and he can't disguise that he thought Bill was going to be a young fellow. My da tries to stand up but I guess he's too taken aback, he starts shivering more than usual and sits down again. "Bill," I say, "this here's my father, who I don't think I told you about." Bill is seventy-one with a few teeth missing himself, so they make quite a pair.

The man is standing outside a bedroom door in a hall lit by the overhead light from the kitchen that's throwing shadows up the stairs. In front of his bedroom, in the puddle of dingy light, he slumps, shirtless. He's small, no taller than I am, has a thin kind of body, but not wiry; his shoulders are curved and soft as a woman's and his skin is very white. He has some long brown hairs on his belly and his lower arms. He has been drinking, which he usually does in the evenings, only tonight he's in worse shape; he started to barbeque us some hamburgers, wearing his chef's hat, the white puffy kind, and singing and not paying enough attention. The fire leapt out of the barrel barbeque and he had to step all over the flying shreds of unburnt papers on the flagstone patio (the flagstones are new), which blackened a few of them and my mother was very angry. Although just to look at her you wouldn't have known it, exactly. You might have felt it. Anger comes rolling off her in waves.

It's chilly out in the hall, and to get into his bedroom he has to beg. "Mommy?" he says, rubbing a hand over his little potbelly. His belly looks like a growth above his thin legs, pooching out, pooching out we used to say, over his belt and under the slight concavity of his chest. He is trying again. Scratch, scratch he goes with his fingernails, trying to be cute by doing like our pussycat, Midnight, does. Then he sniffles, loud enough so she has to hear. "Mommy?"

Somebody's watching him. He knows it, raises his face a bit, catching the little light there is, and covers his face with his arm. It's dramatic and pitiful and I hate her. He makes me want to cry.

I feel sorry for him and with my mind climb inside him and look out through his eyes. I am him, so drunk I don't feel ashamed of myself, just goosebumpy on my upper arms that I start rubbing briskly, which upsets my balance and I teeter, hit the door with my forehead and stay there. "Crud," I say. "Come on, Mommy, come on for Moses' sake." I'm dizzy behind my eyes which is a sure sign it's working, all that booze; as long as the dizziness stays and doesn't move down to my belly and make me sick, I don't mind. I can lie awake on a propped-up pillow, eyes open in the dark, and still snore so she thinks I've passed out. (She likes that, I think. She'll say, Oh, you passed out again last night; say it with that look, a snake spitting venom into the coffee she's pouring from the automatic pot I bought her for her birthday. Oh, you'll need lots of this, she says, pushing the cup and saucer my way. Don't slurp, she'll say, reminding me of when I poured coffee into the saucer when we were at a restaurant which we don't do very often, and so what happened was a big disappointment to her. I was telling a story about people I come from in the South, how they do things, but Mommy didn't hear that part, she only saw me slurping and she rose from the table and called for her coat. I had to stumble along behind, my tie soaked with coffee which happened when I shoved back the chair fast so as not to lose her, and then I really was a mess, which is what she said, You-are-a-mess, through clenched teeth, when we got out on the street. I could have sweet-talked my way out of it, but unfortunately I was having trouble with my words.) I don't pass out, though. Something in me wakes up when the rest of me needs to sleep, and although I look asleep, inside I am on the ball and keeping watch.

A squeak from my door that I've been leaning against sets me back to myself, looking at my da across the hall, my heart whammering in my ears like after running fast a long way. He kicks once against his own door and whispers something I don't hear. Then he's quiet. I start back to bed and realize he's in my room. My feet stick to the floor in a cold sweat. He smells. His eyes are red-rimmed and sad. He says, "Go get in bed, now, Harriet, and get under the covers. Do what your da tells you."

And I do, I'm ten years old.

It went on for a few years. He'd come in and lay himself down beside me and use me as a post, pretty much like some dogs do on a person's leg, or even I've seen them use legs of a chair. He never did anything nasty, never touched skin. He just put his hand on the mound that was my groin, and later on my tits, and then told me to lay still, lay still, don't move, don't move and he would rub up and down on my thigh through the covers. Now, knowing more about these things, I realize his underpants must have been goopy but he would just get up and leave quietly; he never showed me his thing.

Tonight we eat in the kitchen, as Bill and me are accustomed to doing, and my da eats more than his share; you can see he was hungry. We have zucchini bread with fresh whipped cream and honey on it for dessert. At half-past eight Bill leads him upstairs, using the kerosene lamp, a habit for no reason; there's plenty of electricity here, we're not so far off the beaten track. But he's been doing it that way, lights out at seven, for umpteen years and it's his business. We go to our rooms early and in the beginning, if I'd turn on the reading light beside my bed, Bill'd not say a thing, but gradually I came to respect his ways and he mine and so if I have reading to do, I do it by kerosene lamp and let the neighbors think what they will. He settles him in the guest room, although Bill never has guests, his folks and sisters have passed on. Like the other upstairs rooms, there's linoleum on the floor and vinyl draped at the window and the bedding is a thin sheet and an Army blanket and a pillow about the size of a healthy cabbage. There's a chest to put your clothes in, if you can get the drawers to pull out straight, and they're lined with newspapers, old ones, some from WWII and delicate as old lace.

I hear Bill telling my da how to do the lamp, while I wash the dishes in the old tin tub, using a candle or two; I know my way around now. Then I scrub my hands with Lava soap and a brush and go up for the night. Bill says, "Goodnight, Harriet," and I answer, "'Night, Bill," and he says, "Call me now," and I say, "I will," like we've been doing ever since it was apparent my time was coming. It's like that T.V. family, the Waltons, that everybody was watching so intently for a time, and it's goofy, that calling back-and-forth from room to room but it's so peaceful, too, your heart could lurch. My da says nothing, but I hear him anyway, listening.

Maybe it was having my da in the house that makes me not fall asleep, maybe it was the baby kicking, shifting inside me, and about time, turning head downwards, readying to make an entrance. I hope so, there's something so lonely inside me for that baby it's hard to breathe sometimes, if I let my thoughts go with it. I wanted something to hold and my arms ached in the night. I figured it was Nature's way of helping you let go of the comfort of that padded pa-whumpity-thump deep inside you, because after a time, you want it to quit, you'd go through anything to rid yourself of the burden and its secrets; you want whatever it is in the light, so you can see it and get your hands on it.

Through the pink curtain, there's not much moon, hardly a sliver across my cold floor. I have a throw-rug, one of those homey braided things, that I ordered through Sears and it helps, that first shock when you're sitting on the edge of the bed on an icy morning. It's got so I wear socks to bed now, thick ones like the road crews wear, cotton and wool blend with a red band across the top. My circulation seems to have slowed down all through me, except for my belly where the baby feels warm, a mix of earth and fire.

The clock ticking on the bedside table says three when I hear the padded footfalls in the hall. I listen for Bill – he pees in the night and you can always hear it hit the water with a splash, he's been a bachelor all his life – but it isn't Bill, and the creepy feeling on my neck says I'm right. Then I remember my da and it's him, in a strange house, up roaming. Since my mother remarried, he's not been able to get a grip on himself; he slid from head caretaker in a high school to a part-time night watchman, if he's working at all.

He says something, but I can't hear it and before I think to stop myself, I start across to the door. An odd whispering comes through, like something you'd see in a Jack Nicholson movie, as if the door itself is talking to me. My heart is thumping through the big blue vein I've seen pictures of, that carries blood to the little one; the thumping moves my belly. I can't open my mouth and say anything, nothing comes to my brain. My mind dashes out, into the cold hall, edges of linoleum lifting from the old pine floor, to where my da stands barefoot, but I can't do it, can't get inside; instead, I glimpse us, my da and me, foreheads pressed either side of my door. Like listening to the past so still and deep, no words at all, except the one he's saying. "Mommy," he says. I hear it this time. I brace my hip and shoulder against the door, because Bill and me have no need for locks. My belly lies sideways so that if my da decides to stoop and listen, he can hear his grandbaby's heartbeats. Other than the racket inside my head, there's no sound; it's so quiet you can hear the new fridge, a self-defroster, click on. I know his forehead is pushing on my door, I feel it, and his hand is on the knob, throbbing to turn it. I've seen it before, that exact scene, him on my mother's door, afraid to discover it locked. He would wait and breathe and breathe and turn and cross the hall, to me.

At breakfast my da cocks his head sideways and gives me a little wink. Then he raises his arms up slow like someone about to receive a blessing, you see them on T.V., and his wrist bones come out of his sleeves. His hands are thin, the skin stretched smooth and oddly hairless, slightly reddened, like maybe psoriasis healed up. He raises his arms to me and something in me rushes out to him, bawling like a baby.

But there's something niggling in the back of my brain, something I can't quite get my finger on, and then I think of it. When I was twelve and just becoming sexy in the naive way girls have and my da was in, rubbing on me, his hand on a tit but not massaging it, just holding, he always was polite, I pulled down the elastic on my summer nightgown and handed him one. I don't know what I thought would happen, I didn't consider. He opened his mouth automatically, I could see his face turning, glancing up at me from where he was settled against me, head at armpit level, left leg sprawled over my legs under the covers; face turning toward the flashes of headlights passing outside, his eyes

dark, and he opened his mouth and took in my nipple and began sucking. Then he shifted his body and held my tit in both hands, kneading
it like a kitten without claws, and used his tongue in a way that later I
would know to be like a baby does, that whole-jaw sucking movement,
tongue curling around the nipple. It felt good, that warm, wet tugging,
the few times it went on.

Remembering makes me blush and I open the door of the wood
stove to check the morning muffins. I fuss with coffee and mugs and
get the fresh cream we trade with a neighbor for, while I sort myself
out. It becomes clear in me I don't want him around when my baby is
born, I don't want him even in the same county. I take a breath. "I
know how it looks, big house and all," and shake my head no.

His eyes water up, but I've seen it before.

Not that old or that young, either, I've done my share of moving
around. I knew my da had come up on the bus because he smelled like
it. Buses smell like green disinfectant and sometimes, if the bus has
come a distance, like dried urine that the cleaners always miss. Buses
smell cloudy, the air thick with breath from body-insides and worn-
down ideas stroking around inside heads; and all it takes is one smoker
to get the rest of them going and then it gets in the air conditioner system and stays. That's what he smelled like, and slightly fishy, too, like
somebody wearing his clothes too many days.

I used to get on a bus and go, get off, eat in the cafe attached to the
station and climb on again. A bus breathes with people, usually poor,
going where they've been called to: a dying, a funeral, a surgery, a sickness, sometimes a wedding; or looking for a job, a town to live in where
you belong, a man, a woman; sometimes looking for a lost child.
When it rains and the bus is moving smoothly down the road in the
dark, lights from a city or houses darting in and out through streaked
windows and the windshield wipers going slop, slop, it's soothing, cars
passing fast and furious, horns going, like in another world, so far
away on the other side of the thick walls of the bus, while inside you
listen, picking up pieces of quiet conversation and having one of your
own with the old lady beside you who is afraid of dying alone in her

house with no one to find her. She says she picks flowers between watching game shows, playing bridge, and listening to all the Yankee games on the radio. She can tell you the players and their batting averages; she's a fan, sitting in her house having trouble sleeping, afraid she'll have a heart attack in bed and not make it to the living room phone and wondering if she will fall and not be able to get up and wondering how long she could be there before anybody finds her. She has a theory that perhaps sleeplessness has to do with body temperature. Once while visiting overnight her hostess gave her some booties and when her feet were warm, she fell asleep. But probably she fell asleep easily because she was in someone else's house and not alone in her own where she has to stay awake, I think, in order to make sure she can get to the phone if she starts to die. In her own house she has to stay a bit on the alert.

Long distance travel by bus has its own rhythm and thoughts go deep, vibrate to the bus's vibration as it cruises along, beating its scheduled trail around the country. After days and days of deciding which greasy food to eat, of keeping track of your suitcase and tickets and keeping your bottom off of toilet seats and avoiding drunks and other men, your self becomes very compact and floats in and out.

Once drifting on a bus at midnight with lightning off in the distance, voices murmuring, a radio clicking on, the crinkly flipping of a magazine page and me snuggled in with two seats to myself, the driver wheezes into a small town rest stop and speaks over the microphone very politely so as not to wake sleepers. He says not to forget the number of your bus and don't be late getting back and be careful going down the steps and watch your step outside because it's raining cats and dogs. As it turned out, he was from that small town and I stayed. Not for him, personally, but for the kind of place that would raise a man up to be so kind.

I stand in the yard beside the old house that needs paint with the old man who is like my guardian, whose house it is. After supper we came out to watch things and listen, to the birds, the rustling of a cat, the cozy chit-chat of chickens; we look at the clouds and notice the changes in shape. We smell the air full of dying green from the hills, slopes cooling as the season shifts gears into what we hope will be Indian summer. We look at the garden and notice the winter squash blossoms that are new since yesterday. Bill's not had a family, not even been married, but he's game and says it's never too late. Last year he bought a whole side of beef for the freezer, thought he was just foolish and not foresighted.

I stand in the yard that's big and flat and thick with grass and watch the sky. I would like to remember my da like people do in the T.V. commercials for the phone company: a soft-focus old fellow, white of hair and bright of spirit, who would fill you full of sweet memories, that you would want to phone right now. With my da, though, I tried to ignore him drunk and avoid him sober and all the time I was busy doing that, I was watching him and letting him into me; like seepage in a basement, he got in.

Already my tits are oozing. It's going to be an affair to beat all when I've got my little suckling and I know things now and I'm not budging from this town, this land, this spot. If you were looking down from the big house further up the hill, or were a tourist driving by, you might see us just standing here for a time, looking at the sky and hills, but mostly standing, holding down this corner of the earth, holding tight, keeping it quiet and calm, so that you'd be free to move into the fast lane with your headlights on and horn blaring.

Grounding

Ginger Dawn, who is seven now and just full of it, is down the road picking on some chickens. I am on the veranda, reading an eviction letter written by some lawyers in Seattle, Washington. I glance out at the old Gravenstein tree that was split by lightning this past spring, right after Bill died. The grass has grown around it and needs cutting but the mower quit and I'm not mechanical. It's still sad to see the tree there, gnarled and sundered, its trunk burnt on one side. Two weeks back, late in July, three of its branches, one up high like a one-armed man waving and the others lying on the bright grass, sprouted tart little green apples, too soon, but they had to hurry, I guess, attached to no roots. In the fall I plan to get out the chainsaw and cut firewood.

I inspect the writing again. Lawyers use so many words that a person doesn't understand, you have to hire one of them just to read a letter. There are nephews, which I know of, two of them, and Bill's house and land are theirs, as next of kin. Unless there is a proper will. They are giving us six weeks to leave. They say that much time is a courtesy of the owners.

My copper-haired girl comes bawling along the road, holding her finger out. She's spied me on the veranda and carries on louder, then stands howling at the gate waiting for me to go down and unlatch it for her, which I do but I am not happy about it, having things on my mind.

Her nose is making bubbles and she's spluttering about the chickens who attacked her, especially Bloody Mary, the old hen who loves her least. They run free, those chickens, which nobody seems to care about once gardens are in and seedlings are ankle-high. I can't fathom why she is having an ongoing match with a chicken, but she is, trying to tame it, so she says. There is a tiny nip at the end of her finger, and you wonder what it is in a child that knows just when to drive you nuts, when you least need it.

The letter starts to shake in my hand. It's as though I had nearly seven years of peacetime and now, during the last three months, my life has broken out in war.

Ginger Dawn senses something and startles back but not before I grab her, crinkling the letter. My temper is frayed as the rope binding the truck door shut. "You deserve whatever that chicken did," I hear myself say, yanking her arm, and I say, "How many times do I have to tell you?" and then I punch her, biff, right in the chest. She whimpers and curls up and rolls across the grass and lies still. I'm afraid I've knocked the wind out of her or worse, and begin calling to God, like you do when you think your child is hurt or in trouble of some kind, and tripping over myself, drop to my knees beside her.

She's down there giggling and I think I will wring her neck some-day, but in the meantime she makes me cry, and laugh both, and I hope Alma isn't watching from her place across the road or she will think we are crazy. And I say, "You just wait til Bill gets hold of you," and before the words are halfway out, I know I really am crazy, because Bill has been dead since May and I keep forgetting, even with the letter in my hand.

I tuck it in my apron pocket and reach out to Ginger Dawn. In the house I put a nice big Popeye BandAid on her finger where Bloody Mary bit her, then head to the kitchen where I intend to fix her favorite, popcorn that has melted cheese on it. But before the kernels are in the pan she is kicking her feet against the table leg and on her face is the pout that I am so tired of. "No, I don't want that," she says. She has a high-pitched nasal voice, swallowed up into her nose where there isn't room for it. "You always make that when you're trying to get me on your side again and make me forget that you're mean and I hate you. You hit me." I turn from the stove, the pot with sizzling oil still in my hand, and see that the idea is taking root in her. "You HIT me!" she starts in and the stuffing goes right out of me. I am raw, and my patience is as thin as the paint on the wall. I slap the pan down on the stove and flicks of oil splatter onto my arm but I can't even muster the strength for an ouch; it seems I deserve the pain, I deserve it all. I click off the propane burner and wait long enough to hear the windy little flutter it makes as it goes out. All the while Ginger Dawn is raving about having been BEATEN BY MY OWN MOTHER. I turn on her and grit my teeth and snarl and mean it, "You better get out of here, you better run for your life," and her eyes get big and she pushes the chair from the table, screaking the floor, and she does, she runs for her life.

It's sad we have come to this and her just barely seven. I am left to snivel like an old woman into the sink.

Cemetery Road is lined by trees, poplar and ash, and it's straight-arrow uphill when you're past the one curve. At the crest are the Catholics and the Protestants, separate, and an unmarked section off in the weeds for the Neithers. When the funeral's big, when the mayor's son went at too young an age, from leukemia, cars tilt into the ditches on either side of the road for half a mile. There's not much said here when a person dies, and for Bill Perkins it was the same: He was born in this town, and gave a helping hand to it and lived here most of his life except when he went to the city of Seattle to try bookkeeping in his youth and then he came home, to be with his friends and the community. An unmarried man, he left no wife or children but would be remembered by all.

When the preacher got to that point Alma, who is in her late seventies but won't say exactly, peered over her shoulder at me, gave me a severe stare, no mercy in it, kind of gloating and sly. She was wearing a cloche-type hat left over from the forties or before. She has a bit of a hump on her back, and her chin, below a collapsed mouth from bad dentures, juts out same as Mammy Yokum's. She's my neighbor and we have had some dealings, partly, I think, because she had her eye on Bill all her maidenly life. She thinks I am a Jezebel of some kind. I'm young, by her standards, though not comely, by anybody's, kind of squat and square and no-necked, but Ginger Dawn is a beauty, a cinnamon-colored girl in some light, rich cream in others. The way the cedars and alders shadow on her at the cemetery, she looks lightly dusted with cinnamon, she looks like a native to these hills or maybe the plains, she looks like someone I never knew and yet familiar at the same time. Alma always resented Ginger Dawn, the very fact of her; and I always suspected she suspected that Bill was the father of my girl, and for my sake, I wished he were; I'd know who her da was in that case.

Alma's grandniece Leslie, who is fourteen, gave me the eye, too, but for a different reason. She was staying in the room in Alma's house that used to be mine, when I first arrived in town, fresh off the bus, and Alma took me in.

There were some flowers in the church, the Methodist ladies saw to it even though it was hard on some of them; they had to forget Bill's six years with me. They looked right through me and made the arrangements, and it was only on the phone to the church rectory when one of them said everything'd been taken care of that I found out it had; Bill's family, after all, were among the town founders, she said, leaving me with nothing but oh. I sat in the back of the church. There was no family for the front pew, Bill's sisters had died, and the two nephews couldn't come for the funeral. They will be the heirs, Alma said. She walked across the road and leaned over my wire fence to tell me. What she meant was, I would get the boot.

At that time Leslie had spiky hair, the tips orange. Her face was pudgy and pale and close up I saw she applied some kind of whitening powder, for the Munster Family look, I guess, on afternoon re-runs. She had dark eyes, rat's eyes I thought at first, something shifty and sinister running past in her glance, your spine gave a tingle when she looked at you. But in town I heard she was a kid who'd had a hard time. She was at Alma's, had arrived in January, because of some family trouble of the unmentionable kind, it was hinted, and I didn't care to know what.

At first she kept pretty much to herself. The kids here dabbed a little gel in their hair and wore ugly T-shirts and one girl went in for spiked heels at school, but Leslie stood out as something different. You would think that her looking so city, as we say here, would have made her popular, but it didn't. There was something dark about her, something hidden that you didn't want to get close to. But after a while she started hanging on my fence and watching while I shoveled snow off the walk and gradually I saw her for the unhappy girl she was and we took to talking.

One day she dropped in while Bill was down at the hardware store, working on a heat vent problem. She already had sweat glistening on the fine hair of her upper lip, which I might have paid attention to, had I known then what I know now. But perfectly normal she came round back and thumped at the door using the side of her fist, and walked in before I had a chance to invite her, dropped her books on the floor and threw herself at a kitchen chair. Then she fell across the table, arms splayed, because she had a dramatic nature. When she lifted her head she said, "I need some weird clothes from the old days, for social studies. They're doing a project." She generally said "they" although it was her class that was doing the project and she'd been at Towne School for three months. But "they're doing a project," she said, "you got any stuff in the attic like old attics are supposed to? You got any Coke?" I did, of course, for her, although I kept Ginger Dawn away from it for the sugar. Alma's dead set against it, caffeine's what causes the young to be wild, and she might be right, I couldn't say.

I stopped kneading the rolls, wiped my hands on my apron and took Leslie upstairs. In the hall I stood on a stool to tug the rope dangling from the pull-down stairs which led to the attic. The attic had a window at the far end, partly covered in yellowed and brittle plastic that was ripped. Motes of dust floated in the air. Leslie was taller than me, she couldn't stand quite straight even at the peak. There were boxes of Bill's things, his sisters' things, too, from the signs of it, and the usual, a cot frame, a mattress on its side, what looked like old vacuum cleaner hoses, but what caught my eye was a bedside lamp that had a broken stained glass shade. For an attic it was surprisingly tidy, which was Bill's way, and swept. Leslie began digging in a couple of boxes and tossing clothes and I didn't say anything. As a rule too much was said to her, I figured, you could see it when she automatically narrowed her eyes as soon as you looked at her with the intent of opening your mouth, because she knew some correcting would come out.

When I turned back from studying the lamp, considering if it could be mended, she'd stripped off her sweatshirt and slipped out of her calf-length black knit skirt. She was still wearing heavy socks, bobby sox they were called in my day, and black and white Oxfords, but other than that, she was stark naked. She cocked her head on her shoulder and one side of her mouth raised while her eyes pinned me staring at her. She had the tits of a girl, and although they were full they didn't hang as mine always had. All over she was smooth and rubbery-looking, dewy I guess you'd say; her skin was like an old painting where the women were full and fleshy but not rippled by cellulite, or blubbery. "Oh, boy," she said, "oh, God," and before the moan escaped her mouth, she had the mattress flipped down and herself thrown upon it. Puffs of dust rose and settled around her. For a second I glimpsed her full bottom before she flipped like a fish onto her back and ran her tongue along her lips, something a child would do who'd seen movies too old for her, something she fancied was sexy, which made me laugh, a little.

"Humor me," she said and pulled a tit. The nipple, a light pink one but fair-sized, stood upright. By this time I was on my knees beside the mattress, shaking my head no, but looking at her body, when she said, "Aw, go on, just stick a finger up me, slow, just let it sit, no big deal." She was like a big pink baby as I gazed down on her, and I had to give her what she needed, for it was need I sensed in the close, dry air and the feeling, too, that she would scream and howl if I denied her. And so I used the middle finger, the one as kids we had dubbed "bad," and pushed it slowly through the matted hair. The lips of her closed around my finger while the rest of her stayed still, staring at me mysterious and cloudy-eyed like an infant; yet this infant had managed to entrap me, and I kept moving my finger in deeper, aware of her inner muscles clinching, nibbling, as she worked herself against it, her body quiet as though I would punish her if she moved is what I thought, and she never took her eyes off my face. I pushed a little more, to the part that felt like plastic packing bubbles if I concentrated on it, and I was. She pulled her tit, rapid little movements, she favored the left one, and I bent over her a little further and took it in my mouth and tongued it and in moments she burst on me, my finger wet with her. It was in that instant I recognized that I had turned into a pervert. I pulled my finger that was being held by suction, out, fast. She said, "My dad was never nice like you," and I thought I would throw up.

Until then I had been living the life of Riley.

But afterwards, through the house was the feeling of broken glass, the shards all over the place and me doing a bit of secret bleeding, too ashamed to speak. I couldn't step anywhere in that house that had been so cozy, quiet and safe, without guilt so sharp my body felt cut. And, too, Bill was tired that spring in a way I hadn't seen him before, sitting in his favorite rocker, the padded one with maple claws that his hands fit comfortably over, and watching a lot of T.V. in the evenings, when usually he would be in the shop sanding a cedar chest or inventing a new tool by putting together odds and ends of old metal pieces from this and that. He worked slow, an idea forming in his mind like the natural blossoming of a flower in its time; you never hurried Bill and you never said you had to have something repaired in a hour. He would just glance down at you, he was tall and had long arms and big, knotty hands that hung uneasily at his sides as though he never learned what to do with them when they weren't mending or making, he would glance down and not even smile. His eyebrows would raise slightly and then he'd gaze off, over your head or to one side, as though sizing up the hills themselves and then he'd say, "Looks like rain," or "Mighty nice day," and I had seen it so often, that person in a hurry would turn and look where Bill was looking and the frown would fall from their face because it was like they saw what Bill saw and time was the least of it.

The once I had surgery, they wheeled me into a tiled room, strapped my arms at the wrists, fastened a mask across my nose and mouth and forgot to turn on the oxygen. My eyes were bugging in my head and my back was arching before the doctor noticed. I know because something of me was watching from a corner of the ceiling. I heard his "oh" near my right ear and the click that followed. But the image of those seconds, or however long it was, that my life hovered at the ceiling took months of nightmares to pop into my conscious mind as something that had actually happened. It took that long, I think, because it was shocking to my system to see my body as a thing lying on a table, a thing without me in it, like a shell among many on a beach, not that much different from the rest; except in the tiled room, theirs were filled with selves and mine wasn't.

With Leslie I did what I did, my eyes wide open, so I couldn't say I was driven by grief or loneliness or any of the usual. Maybe it isn't natural for a thirty-seven year old woman to live without sex, but I was feeling fine and suddenly there she was, that tallish big girl, dark eyes gazing at me, a helplessness in her wanting any kind of attention. The fact that I was old enough to be her mother shamed me. That old but couldn't keep in my mind what was right. If we had been school girls I could mentally wiggle my way out of it, but I was a molester like the rest of them. And like the rest of them I would never do it again, I was so filled with shame at myself. And like the rest of them I wondered, if she were to lay her body down for me, I wondered would I do it again.

I couldn't look Bill in the eye and it wasn't because we were lovers. He was twice my age and some, he was like my guardian, he cared for me like a daughter, in the right way, in the way a man should care for his daughter, leaving her body alone. And I felt I had blasphemed under his roof. Ours was an odd relationship, I know I would think so, standing on the outside. We were easy together and left each other privacy while sharing things like chores and meals and a sip of Scotch now and then. "What's wrong, Bill?" Ginger Dawn would say during this period, rocking in her socked feet on the linoleum. "What's wrong, Mom?" Or she'd say, "What's going on, guys?" Then she took to punching us, whamming Bill in the shins with whatever sharp toy was at hand and butting me in the belly with her head. She was a pain and I walloped her more than once, but she came out fighting, every time. Bill didn't know what to do and neither did I. We ignored her, shooed her from the room whenever she came wearing that cross expression on her face. In the last days of his life we weren't talking, much, although he would look over his big coffee mug, regard me in that waiting way he had, and I couldn't meet his eyes, I always came up with kitchen tasks to tend to.

But of course I couldn't tell anybody what I'd done and I doubted Bill would ever be able to imagine it if I had. And I couldn't just carry on, in the simple ways of before: work and easy chat and playing with Ginger Dawn and reading by lamplight. And so we were estranged, for the first time in our six years and some together, and when Bill made seventy-eight and a week, he passed away.

It was peaceful and quick, in the night while he was sleeping, not awake thinking of what had gone wrong, I hope. It wouldn't be like Bill to worry, but I knew he'd put it through his mind. "You're young," he said after supper once and I shook my head, guessing what he was leading to, and I was stymied as to what to say next, still am. But I cried for all I could have said, about the good things and him, instead of being wound tight in on myself, spun like a cocoon, suspended high above the body I couldn't bear to look at, what it had done, and distant from them, too, Ginger Dawn and Bill; but I didn't see that part, until too late.

All that while I had been avoiding Leslie like the plague. After Bill died and I saw her at the funeral alongside Alma, there was something even sadder in her eyes, and Alma tugging on her jacket as though spiking a horse to get a move on. "It's nothing bad," Leslie said one day when I passed her in the aisle of the Safeway and all I could feel was my finger, wet.

When the nephews decide to move, they move fast.

It's the next Tuesday after the letter and I'm elbow deep in cherry-port preserves that I sell through the local craft shop and even in the gourmet section of a store in Clinton, fifty miles north. Fifty-two pint jars are sterilized and ready, lined up on the counter, the stove-top, the table, even on top of the refrigerator, and bubbling in a canning pot is the first stage, the port jelly. The sour cherries are piled in a clean bucket, split and partly mashed. Someone taps on the kitchen window. When I raise my head, he flashes a lawyer's paper and grins, very friendly, so as to make me trust him, I guess, but I don't, instantly. That big grin seems worked on.

He's not what I pictured. A fellow straight from Seattle I supposed would be in a suit, I had an evil mustache on him, too, at least a lawyer wearing sharkskin I was hoping for. But Dwayne Smith, that was his name, was fat in the middle, wearing wrinkled old cords, and he'd driven across in a pick-up so small it puzzled me how he squeezed in, much less moved his foot on the pedals. He was standing on the service porch sweating like a pig, rolls of fat ringing his neck. You could see a little dirt oozing out. He had smallish eyes, plain blue, and was balding with wisps askew in the heat.

He was so normal-looking my heart sank.

After I washed up and settled him in the parlor, he drank a pitcher of homemade lemonade and referred to me as "ma'am." He wouldn't call me Harriet, no ma'am, he was on business to see the house, getting ready to sell, and much appreciated the refreshment. He sounded more and more like somebody in that old T.V. show, "Green Acres," and it was hard to stay cheerful, because nobody was going to side against him. What I mean is, I had a distant dream that everybody in town would help me keep Bill's place. What I mean is, they'd choose me over some slick and absent nephews. And their choosing would make it legal.

He says, "Sorry about that ol' letter. Them's lawyers for you, threatening before they have to." He shrugs. "Uncle Bill was mighty fond of you and your little girl. She's a honey. Hair such as that's rare. Maybe I could help you out, help you find a new place."

He's trying to sidetrack me so that the threat in what he's saying almost passes me by. "What kind of work you say you do?"

"Little this, little that. I'm kind of handy like Uncle Bill."

I suppose to him I look dumb, squat and plain, more brawn than brains; he probably heard about me before he came out. A handyman, my eye. His hands are pudgy and soft and it doesn't take but a glance to see his nails aren't embedded with the combination of dirt, paint and grease a real handyman has and it doesn't matter if you use Lava soap or not. His brother and him probably spent a day or two playing Halloween, fixing Dwayne Smith in this get-up, solely for my benefit.

It's embarrassing showing him around because Ginger Dawn is not the neatest person and then we get to my room and I guess I'm not either. His face doesn't change, he scans and nods and sometimes smirks, or maybe I imagine it, and when we're back in the parlor he's shaking his head and muttering, "Old house. Needs lots of work. Windows gotta be bigger, bay'd be nice in the living room. New kitchen. Veranda a shipwreck," taking notes in one of those steno pads.

When he looks up, he doesn't bother to grin. He's got dollar signs in his eyes, he's already calculating costs.

I suddenly see that I'm not needed here and for the first time I wonder what the heck is going to happen in my life next.

After the preserves, my heart is still so unsettled I dig out the needlepoint footstool cover I've been working on for years, I hate needlepoint, and make myself do a bit, sitting in Bill's rocker and glancing now and again at the mantel where his pension checks that have come by mistake are propped and mock me, because I am trying to hold off getting a job until school starts. I'm rocking back and forth listening to the squeaks on the slick wood floor and getting madder and madder. We were his family, I always thought, but he left no will that I can find. I begin the search again. You can get sort of single-minded, looking for something you don't even know if it's there.

It is no fun being the age when paper takes over your life. The searching for it is bad enough, but as the days tick by like time bombs it comes clear that I have to do something, either pack or stick. There are two lawyers in town and I go to the oldest one, I figure he will have heard everything under the sun already, and tell him my story, which is none of his business, but that's the law. It's possible I have a claim on the estate which I think at first means the house but doesn't, necessarily, and in any event, if I decide to go on, there will be forms and papers to fill out and file and claims and possibly court. In the meantime he could send in something to keep them from selling the house. My chances, though, aren't good. He tells me straight out. It would help if there was a scribbled note or a witness to his intent to bequeath the house to me, if he said it. Even if I could swear he said it would help. But I can't.

On a windy awful morning when I think the whole garden is going to blow down and Ginger Dawn is very loudly wanting to go to town for donuts and has gone so far as to stamp her feet from the safety of her room, I find weevils in my bag of flour that was going to last us and that's when Leslie comes clumping onto the veranda. She has been away at a Christian youth camp Alma sent her to. Marching into the entry hall, she says, "I know what I'm doing. You act like it's such a big deal but it's not. I'm not a virgin and never was, so who cares?" She's wearing a shirt of Alma's brother who died a few years back, a plaid shirt, patched together by an old man's big, careful stitches. Her hair is cut short, the orange fringe is gone, and her face is bare of make-up; she doesn't look like herself at all.

There's something off about me, I guess, because I don't shush her though she's saying things Ginger Dawn shouldn't hear. Although the likelihood of Ginger Dawn hearing anything isn't good just now, the way she's throwing things around in her room.

It is almost a week since the lawyer and this morning I woke early, thinking. The lawyer made me repeat anything the nephew said, word for word, to take the measure of my situation, and it's finally today that I hear what Dwayne Smith said about Ginger Dawn and begin to wonder how he knew the color of her hair. Bill must have written to him, I don't know who else would. And if Bill wrote to him, maybe he said about the will and maybe the nephews burned the letter. I have got the whole picture built in my mind of them cackling, if men cackle, and drinking bourbon and poking at the fire.

I used to be a person of principles, but since Ginger Dawn turned animal in what I hope is a phase, I cave in. Leslie's eyes are glinting at me as I yell up the stairs that we're going for donuts. I try to say it with spirit, as though it's my idea.

The wind is high and I have got Leslie by the hand, walking back from town, and Ginger Dawn hanging on to my other. We're sticky from the chocolate coating and sugar sprinkles. Leslie is da-dooing, sounding happy, Ginger Dawn isn't so sure, she's struggling in my grip. "I'm too damn old for hand-holding," she says, sounding not a bit like just-turned seven, "and besides, you're up to something, I know you, Harriet." She must be imitating Leslie; she's never called me by my first name.

"What is it would make you happy?" I demand but don't stop walking.

"None of your cotton candy."

"Why don't you slug her?" Leslie wants to know, still humming, peering round me at Ginger Dawn as though she's a specimen to be squashed. We're panting near the top of the hill, me dragging Ginger Dawn who is squinting nastily, her fuzzy orange hair bobbing on her stalk-like neck, when the wind catches us full-body. The weight of it against the heart of me is too much, and crushing their hands, gathering speed and breaking into a run, I begin pulling them over the crest of the hill, as though they are my wings. Then I leap. Leslie has anticipated me, felt the dip of my arms and comes along, but Ginger Dawn misses it, she's less experienced. Because of her stumbling, Leslie and I are wrenched and almost fall on her, but Leslie is strong and yanks us back, still moving. My grip on Ginger Dawn slips free and the two of us are off, my legs rubbery but fast as scudding clouds anyhow. It's downhill the whole way.

I am laughing, until we get to Alma's garden and herself leaning over the fence, waving a handful of delphiniums and mums, petals flying, which puts the brake on. Her face is red as a beet and she's pointing back up the hill. I let go of Leslie and look, see Ginger Dawn lying spread-eagled on her back in the road, wailing, making a scene all over the world. She has gone too far. My throat is raw. "You take her," I tell Alma, inspiration striking like a bolt of lightning. "You always suspected me and Bill, you take her. You figure her out."

Oh, freedom, I'm off like a shot, pulling Leslie behind me. To the bottom of the road, hang a right, down to a fast walk now and lungs on fire, walking toward the hills and never coming back.

Everyone has a crazy period or two in their life and I am having mine.

When we get to the foothills and into some woods, the wind blowing in the leaves, I press her down and kiss her cheeks as I used to do Ginger Dawn's when she was a baby. Then I kiss her lips that are sticky and sweet with donut sugars. She sticks her tongue in my mouth, which makes me sick it's so sudden and I have to call her off. I lie on top of her and press pubic bones and she gets off on it, as she tends to say, and wraps her legs around my thighs, pinning me, and massages her own breasts while I support myself with my hands, keeping a distance. All the while I'm pressing on her I'm mystified why didn't he leave a will? Or a scrap of paper for me to find? I thought Bill cared about us, I thought we were friends forever. All of a sudden Leslie throws me off. "It isn't working," she says, rolling on the dry ground, her hand holding her crotch. Then she unzips her jeans, shrugs them down her thighs and begs for my finger. I swore I'd never do it again but here I am, about to do it again. But not for love, just pity for myself. And that's what finally makes me cry.

Alma gives me a stony look when I pick up Ginger Dawn before supper. She wouldn't ever understand. All night I turn myself round in slow motion, shake loose my hand from Leslie's soft and sweaty one and fly back up the road to swoop my baby into my arms. I can't explain what possessed me to abandon her, even for a second, for in that second it's possible a car, some car full of teenagers or the brown pick-up of the drunk that lives down the next road from us, could have sped around that corner and killed her lying there shrieking her head off, fool that she is, and my own.

I ease back the lace curtain in the living room and watch Alma in her rose garden, toiling alone, the grey-green house behind her seeming bigger now that Alma's frailer which I hadn't been noticing, thinking of myself all the time. She's going fast, her skin must be bits of chaff in the wind, because it seems every time I look at her, she's smaller.

We used to sit on the veranda shelling peas or husking corn, Alma and me and her younger sister Grace when she was visiting. Then Grace took sick and I had to move out. Grace died of liver cancer, it took her a year, and Alma kept her at home and took care of her. And now the years have gone by and the love of Alma's life, Bill, is dead, oh it was a secret, but everybody knew, as is the way in small towns.

In the months of Grace's slow dying, I moved in with Bill and Alma never forgave me. I didn't do it on purpose, I didn't move in on Bill hoping he would die and bequeath me the place. But because of how we were together, I assumed I would live there all the rest of my life, it never crossed my mind different.

Alma isn't tickled about inviting me in. I stand in the kitchen, awkward and guilty of just about everything, while she sizes me up before leading me into her living room that is so familiar, even after all these years. On bad T.V. nights, we used to set up the bridge table and play cribbage. And once we had a surprise party for Grace. Alma's living room is like a velvet garden, full of deep blues and roses and burgundies and lace things, doilies covering the backs and arms of the furniture, but you don't feel pinched as some doilied rooms make you feel. These doilies are layered and draped by the dozens, and they make you very comfortable.

Except today it's not comfortable for me, listening to her get the tea things and to the ticking of the grandfather clock in the dining room. When at last she hands me tea, she says, "And how is little Ginger?" I see she intends to assume badly of me, as I do myself these days.

I duck my head and try to explain, about the nephews and my worrying and how upset Ginger Dawn's been lately. But Alma, slipping on the glasses that hang on a chain around her neck, reminds me that Ginger Dawn's just a child, as though I needed reminding. But I apologize to her, for my rudeness and the trouble I caused and then I do for her what I forgot with Bill and thank her for helping me out when she did so long ago and yesterday, too, and I thank her for the good times we had together.

Her thin lips twist. She is wearing pink lipstick that has run into the cracks around her mouth. "You'll have to excuse me, I have things to do," she says, and I am pricked somewhere near my heart. For all I think I am independent of her and everybody, Alma is still my closest tie to Bill. She knew him first, she knew him longest.

But when I leave I feel a little better, because I see that by her not treating me kind, she will have to forgive me in the end. Her guilt will get her.

The next evening another thunder and lightning storm hits us, it has been the wettest August in anybody's memory, and Ginger Dawn and I drag foamies and sleeping bags onto the veranda and watch the storm through the wood-slat railing, lying on our sides. The veranda is high enough from the ground so that even when the rain slants from the south and kicks up mudballs in the flower beds we stay dry, the eaves protect us. The jagged spines of lightning thrill her, but she's scared, too, there are solid cracks and rumbles of thunder. "Mom," she says and I lift my sleeping bag for her and she scoots from hers to mine. Her body is thin and small but rangy, she's one of those all arms and legs. Instantly she's warm against me, snuggling in, but I draw back in my letting the feeling of her melt me, wondering if I can be trusted, wondering if molesting children is in your genes.

It's like she's a mind reader. "How come you're not friends with Leslie anymore? How come, Mom?" She asks it listlessly, as though she expects no answer, certainly no real answer. I don't have one, either. With temptation the only thing I know to do is thwart it, move it out of your path. Leslie has to keep away.

"What would make you happy?" I ask her.

"Bill come back," she says in the baby way of someone younger and I realize she has been left out in the turmoil of Bill's dying; she has been forgotten, when, in fact, it's her who lost the only man she will ever think of as father.

One morning at the end of August Ginger Dawn and I walk up to visit Bill in the cemetery. She carries her little rake and daisies from her garden. She has on a blue and white checkered dress that she's never worn because she hates dresses. In a cemetery on the northern coast of California that I was in once, the wind was so strong if you opened your mouth to take a breath it could lift you upward, sail you off the cliff and over the ocean crashing in a rush below. It was a bone-bruising wind that took your voice away when you tried to shout with joy. Walking there was like being tipsy, off-balance as I was and bashing into tombstones. I imagined ghosts ganging up, to rid me from their place. There are no ghosts around Bill's grave, though, and no wind; it's peaceful here, the leaves are beginning to turn, a bit early, but the sun is bright. Ginger Dawn, after tucking her flowers in the earth, stands solemnly, her hands folded in front of her, her long legs straight. I will be happy to hear her laugh again.

Heading home I tell her about the cemetery and the wind, I want her to understand wind and a bit about the day I left her in the road, what I thought I was trying for. I always suspected that with a gust of wind at your front and a good running leap, you could suspend yourself between sky and earth, hold on in space, if you could keep your mind still enough to let it happen.

The beatitude of a place is what I'm thinking about, its deepness and your attachment. The beatitude has to do with a foundation, like on a house, but of some invisible kind, something despite appearances and some people not liking you, some ease you feel standing in a particular spot. In my mind, as we walk, I pack up and leave. I put Ginger Dawn's toys in the cedar hope chest Bill made for her when she was born and I pack my old knapsack, the one I used on the road for quite a while, and I lock the door and throw the key in the lilacs growing in front of the veranda to make it at least a little hard for the nephews and I vanish down the road, Ginger Dawn skipping in front of me, the sash on her dress bouncing.

Common law certainly isn't what it used to be. Bill and me weren't married, even by common law, but it's the only pigeonhole anybody could fit us into that would make any sense to them. What the lawyer termed "the deceased's intention" wouldn't help in my case either. Did Bill ever say, Harriet Mary Dawn, I want you to have my house and land? Of course he did not. And I figure it's because he was far past thinking of any of it as his, as something he possessed. He didn't have a mortgage to remind him of the frailness of ownership. And if he had said it, to make the words any good he would have had to stop traffic on Tenth Street and announce it in front of witnesses. Solid community types. No fly-by-nights. No vagrants. Nobody who showed up on a bus hauling just a knapsack and maybe already pregnant, maybe not, for all they knew. As for that business, I think Bill liked that nobody knew for sure. "You think old Bill coulda – ?" He overheard years ago on a Friday, the day he goes – used to go – to town for the mail and Pablum for Ginger Dawn, he heard it in the Seniors' Hall. He waited years to tell me, though, until in the evening after Ginger Dawn's six-year-old birthday party where kids had run though the place like a herd of cattle. He told it to me after she was asleep and before I started on the serious clean-up, while we were sitting, resting, at the lino-topped table in the kitchen, just the kerosene lanterns on. Blushing, his eyes not glancing in my direction, he told me. Because I could see his pride, I did what I seldom had: reached out my hand and clamped it top of his, but only for second, I didn't want to scare him to death.

I leave Ginger Dawn in the yard playing under the squash leaves with her miniature dolls and go inside the house. As I walk around, touching things, my eyes fall on our bus tickets lying on the mantel and I let my gaze flicker past, my hands busy touching. It is your touching things over the years that makes them really yours and the feel of them reminds you about yourself. The backs of my legs recognize the prickles on the old arm chair, my hands have memorized the shape of the faucets, my feet the slight slant of the kitchen floor. My marks are on this house and heaven knows, Ginger Dawn's too.

In Bill's room I tiptoe, as though someone might hear me, from dresser to closet to peering under his bed. From a cigar box under the old-fashioned washstand I finally gather an unfinished note to his older sister that was never mailed and a list of contents of the shed. I pull down the stairs to the attic and hole up in there and start writing dusty bequeathing notes to myself signed by Bill. They'll probably find me out, but it'll take time, and besides, as a kid I always was good at copying my mother's name. I figure you are given nothing in this life, you have to fight for it all. And I'm stubborn, I know myself for it.

Flight

Butterflies always seem free and easy, even after I learned the truth of them. In part I guess I figured they were free because most likely they didn't recall what they were before they had wings, before they began their fluttering. Their brains couldn't be big enough to remember personal past events or to keep track of what happened to them next. Each stage must seem new and each moment a beginning and at the same time all that is. I didn't exactly know why I was talking butterflies with a boy wearing black and enough grease on his hair to lube the truck out back, but there was something about him, more than the ugly bruise on his face, that made me do it. We were in the mud room, which was chilly and smelled of past-their-prime winter pears brought up from storage, my girl Ginger Dawn, this sixteen-year-old boy and me. His name was Kelly Mangiardi.

The boy had a bruise, mustard-yellow and pea-green, spread along his left temple, which was the cause of what the visit was about. He was running away from home. Ginger Dawn planned to borrow the truck so that she could drive him to Clinton to catch the bus from there. That way, they thought, his dad wouldn't find him if he went hunting. The boy had an old duffel bag at his feet and was wearing jeans with a hole in one knee and a pair of new-looking fake leather cowboy boots that had spurs on the backs of them. He was spindly-legged, his legs were almost bowed, but his arms sticking out of rolled-up cuffs were tanned and muscular, like some men's arms are when you can see how the muscles fold and knit together. Ginger Dawn gave me one of her wrath-of-God looks when I took off on butterflies, but Kelly frowned and studied me as though he was listening. This butterfly business was the closest I came to being religious, and I saved it for special occasions.

Ginger Dawn and this boy had been going together for a month or so. She didn't suspect I knew. Teenagers talking in code on the phone or giggling with their friends thought that your brain was too old to add one and one together. Even when they were reluctantly deigning to have a word with you, in cryptic bits as hard as rabbit poop, they still thought they were keeping secrets.

I began to fuss with the coats on the hooks, as though there was a sudden need to organize them according to seasons, switching gardening jackets and torn windbreakers from one hook to the other while I was thinking and looking him over. He was much taller than I was, but unlike me, he was built slight, and had large, brown eyes, so dark they were almost black and matched his hair. He was the same height as Ginger Dawn in her new high heels, the fire-engine red ones which she must have chosen especially for my benefit, because in them she towered above me more than usual.

Outside, the wind whipped up and banged the gate. The sound was like someone leaving in anger. I sped along in my speech and got to the part about memories and how it is our nature to hold onto them. How we can run but not fly.

The pears were softening and some were mushed into the cardboard of their box. I picked half a dozen good ones to make an ice cream sauce for dessert and handed them to the boy to carry. It was only just after four o'clock in the afternoon, but I said, "I've got a stew," and set off towards the kitchen because I could tell from the circles under his eyes that he was in want of a feed. I couldn't be party to a youngster running from home, even the terrible home of Morris Mangiardi.

My copper-haired girl piped up in that nasal voice of hers. "He's going to miss the bus, Mom, you don't understand the awesome danger he's in. His dad has, like, threatened to do him serious harm." But when he began to follow me, spurs clanking now and then on the wood floor, she shut her mouth.

Kelly put the pears in the colander on the counter and took off his leather jacket and placed it neatly across the back of the chair that I pointed to as his. I put more wood in the stove, because though it was the end of March and bright outside, the wind was cold and I was still wearing two flannel shirts and tattered longjohns under my baggy jeans. Ginger Dawn wasn't about to give in on the use of the truck and while sullenly setting the table, she went on, "I'd use the back roads, nobody'd see. You let me deliver the jam once, in fact you forced me." She was referring to the jams and preserves I was famous for in two counties and the delivery deadline I was hard pressed to meet last fall. Three ladies working and one got flu and that left two. I wasn't thinking about the jam though. As I stirred the lamb stew, I thought a person could really fear for her, a girl that tall and that darn dumb, as though her driving was all we had been standing in the mud room talking about.

Plunking the thick coffee-shop style plates onto the warm wood stove, I gave the boy a quick glance and saw that he was already watching me, already had his dark eyebrows half-raised, waiting to be agreeable. A greasy curl had fallen loose in the center of his forehead, which he did not bother to brush away. He grinned and tucked his napkin into his black T-shirt so it was a white fan down his chest and picked up his silverware and nodded at the picture in "Jack and the Beanstalk", where the giant's holding his fork and knife straight up, that was lying open on the table. Some afternoons I read to a child named John, who was eight and slow in school. Kelly's taking that pose made us laugh. "Oh, you," Ginger Dawn said, poking his arm.

On the shelf above the sink, beside a row of tomato seedlings in their peat pots, was a glass of whiskey that I had been about to start sipping when they showed up. Seeing my girl touch that boy in such a familiar gesture – I felt like a Peeping Tom, seeing what I shouldn't – prompted me to reach for the glass and knock the whiskey back, which was a mistake. It hit the wrong pipe and I choked. In a blink Kelly was patting my shoulder, saying, "There, there, breathe now," kindly, as though he were experienced at this sort of thing, which of course he was. I was managing a hardware store and there was not much you didn't eventually get wind of in a town this size. Morris Mangiardi was a ruffian sort of fellow who occasionally spent nights in the local jail.

Kelly, though, was beginning to remind me of a chameleon I had seen once in the desert. When the tears cleared from my eyes and I turned around, he was already back at the table, grinning and offering his empty milk glass as a thirsty child would. One side of his mouth curled a bit in a grin and he looked sheepish at the same time, as though you could hurt his feelings without half trying. I reached into the cupboard and splashed some Jack Daniels into his glass.

"Geez, Mom, you never let me touch the stuff," whined my girl. She went on a bit, as was her manner, before petering out. Kelly raised his glass in a toast. "To real friends." His expression glazed over in that way that makes eyes shiny as marbles. I thought he was going to cry, but he grinned, then swallowed the whiskey down. Ginger Dawn looked away. I put three steaming bowls of stew on the table and sat. Kelly bowed his head and said, "Sorry hungry children of the world," and tucked in.

By the time they left for the movies, I knew he wasn't going to run away, but I had lost track inside myself of whether that was good or bad. Ginger Dawn was wearing her full lips painted a siren red so they caught your attention first on her face. And he, this Kelly Mangiardi, in the coming dark looked like something wet, right out of the cocoon, its wings pressed tight. Or something sleek and fox-like but wary, maybe one of those foxes used to being hunted by hounds. Or maybe something weaselly, but I missed that part and didn't catch onto it until later. At the time I was concentrating on his cheap pointy-toe boots. I was busy picturing his feet and how they must have been hurting, the baby toes rubbed to blisters, the feet in general kind of pinched and in need of a bath. And I was thinking how ready I was to start running the water.

Sometime after midnight, rocking and nipping at a drink, I was on the veranda, wearing a wool hat and buried in my old down coat, when they came strolling along the road. I wasn't sure what I was doing outside on a moonless night, so cold you could imagine frost on the patch of ground that was lit by the street light at the corner. I think I was pondering my life and the events in it, what had happened by surprise and, looking back, what seemed sensible and to be expected. I was rocking, my hands curled around my arms inside the sleeves of my coat, and thinking about kids and what the world must seem to them. I saw the glint in Ginger Dawn's eyes as they went out the door. To her this straggly, beaten boy was a whirl of possibilities, a mineral lode to be mined. But with that one, she had better be careful or the roof would cave in, the foundations were weak. I knew because I recognized him, I recognized in him what happens to your face after that first drink of the day, how smooth your look gets then and how the frown you have been holding eases away.

I was thinking, too, about my life and this house. It was me who ended up buying the house from Bill Perkins' nephews at an inflated price, but it was okay. I believe that people get theirs in the end, and for the nephews I used to picture the old falling-safe gag from the silent comedies, only they wouldn't escape. They would be a smear on a sidewalk of Seattle and on the front pages of the Seattle Times, the miracle of it, or rather, the not-miracle of it, that the nephews hadn't heard the safe whooshing down on them and that no one on the busy downtown street had given a thought to pushing at least one of them out of the way. Or it might have been a falling tree from someone's rooftop garden that you read about in the people magazines, something, anyway, heavy as hell falling from a penthouse roof, maybe a gnarled exotic tree in a thousand-pound ceramic pot.

I was gazing into the night at the end of another winter and thinking about the seasons, the ribbons of color or no-color that we walk on throughout the year and how our feet are similar to a plant's roots, they attach us to the earth if we stop long enough, as I had done; and that led into thinking of wrist bones, because I could feel mine cold even inside the sleeves, and how they are shaped like nodes of young apple trees. I was thinking about aging, how our fat as we get older is like the too-much in a bountiful garden at the beginning of autumn, when you find twenty squashes you didn't notice you had and wish you didn't; and how our vision becomes blurred as mist on morning hills. As I sat staring out, I saw that the only change in my daily view was the way the sky's light fell on the hills and grass and gardens and the house, through the seasons and depending on the times of day and the particular weather. I was thinking how I was still in my forties and as buried as my old neighbor Alma.

After midnight they came moseying along the road, hanging on to each other. I watched from my distant perch, invisible against the dark house, and stopped my chair rocking so they wouldn't hear.

In the kitchen later, I had my back to them and was busying myself at the double boiler, stirring bittersweet cooking chocolate, fixing hot cocoa they said they didn't want. I had my back to them to give them a chance to wipe the lipstick smears from his face and neck as much as a kerchief and spit would do. They had come onto the veranda on tiptoes and he had removed his leather jacket and was putting it down, behind the broken swing chair where, I noted as I was intently stirring the milk and chocolate, they couldn't be observed from the road. He was patting it as smooth as a jacket would go, when I had seen enough and spoke, because I did not desire to know what they were up to. "Geez, Mom!" Ginger Dawn sputtered. But she couldn't get the usual snarkiness into her tone because, I thought, she was guilty as hell. There was not enough light to see the blush to the roots of her hair, and I was sorry I missed it, but I could sense the heat coming from her face. While she was distracting me, the boy, smooth as silk, had swooped up his jacket and hooked it over his shoulder on a finger as though it were simply a hot night and he'd been casually carrying it that way all along.

There wasn't too much to say and they followed me, as children will do, into the house because none of us knew how else to behave and then they were sitting again at the kitchen table and I was pulling an Aunt Jemima, going on about what to eat and the signs of spring's coming. I heard them at my back whispering and hissing to each other like two snakes and their chairs scraping the floor, and I hummed louder, my heart filled with such meanness as I had not experienced in a long time, which cheered me. I imagined my tidy girl frowning and scrubbing his face, hard, because when I did glance at them again, to bring the steaming mugs to the table, his lips and chin appeared scalded, and along with the awful bruise on his temple, he looked like a fellow who had had one hell of a day. She sat staring at me squinchy-eyed.

As the mug and its melting marshmallow came to his lips, he wobbled. I thought he was spoofing, trying to win me over by saying with his body that the chocolate was so good it knocked him out of his seat. Instead, like an earthquake that takes you a moment to realize you aren't losing your mind or your eyeballs haven't come unhinged, but that the earth itself is unsettled, is how it was, recognizing what was happening to Kelly. He teetered in his chair and his eyes took on a glassy look and then Ginger Dawn fast as lightning reached across and grabbed the mug from his hands a moment before he tumbled onto the floor. I leapt to my feet, banging my chair against the stove. Kelly was stretched out tight. He quivered and writhed, the veins in his neck protruding and his eyes rolling back in his head. Ginger Dawn stepped over my fallen chair and elbowed me clear. She snatched a pot holder from the stove and folded it around the wooden stirring spoon. She pried open his teeth and placed the padded spoon between them. In her efficiency she moved me to think of pioneer women, the ones who came west in covered wagons with their men, the ones who suffered as their babies one by one took sick and died on beds of rags; the ones who hid under those same wagons when Indians attacked, yet who, given a rifle when all seemed lost, shot straight and true. Kelly's back arched, his legs kicked the table and his open hands slammed the floor once and it was over. He rolled onto his side. She took the pot holder and spoon out of his mouth and caressed his sweaty face and smoothed back his hair.

"He has epilepsy, Mom," said my dear girl, using the oven door handle to haul herself to her feet, and bursting into tears, stepped back from my open arms.

Of course you couldn't send a boy home who'd had a fit, been beaten and, in any event, was running away. Ginger Dawn stroked and tickled his cheeks to wake him, but he wouldn't rouse past muttering. Because he was too heavy to lug upstairs, we decided to bed him down in the living room. She directed us how to move him, I was to lift his rear and knees while she had the head and shoulders. We scuttled him through the dining room, into the living room and onto the couch, which was short for his long body and a lumpy thing, but it didn't seem he would mind or notice. By the time she tugged his boots off and patted a blanket over him, he was breathing deeply, lost in sleep. I went straight to the kitchen to have a shot. I was proud of my girl and soon glowing inside.

As I was about to praise her presence of mind, she said, in that flat-footed manner she sometimes got, "You drink too much and don't you be feeding him any more liquor, either." After that kind of remark, which might've well been a sharp whack between the shoulder blades, the one giving it generally marched away, their anger becoming more self-righteous, until by the time they had stomped upstairs and slammed the bedroom door, they were in a real snit. But Ginger Dawn did not move. She had her high heels off, so we were more equal in height, but she did not budge even when I glared into her eyes in the manner that used to scare the pants off her. Her standing her ground and saying what she had said in that tone was a dare to my ears. No words formed in my mouth, but I deliberately reached back into the cupboard and brought out the almost-empty Jack Daniels and placed it on the counter in plain sight of us both. Then I poured myself more than I wanted because there was something mean still in me that had begun earlier in the day. I plastered a smile on my face that I hoped was

serene, and raising my glass to her, nodded my head in a silent toast
and chugged it down. Tomorrow I would have a sick headache, but I
had earned it, it would be mine and worth it, for the glimpse of fury
that passed across her young, tired face, like a storm inside her that she
had swallowed.

To manage a hardware store it's not necessary to be skilled in
do-it-yourself, but you do have to anticipate and match your orders to
sales, read the trades and catalogs, keep your eye on suppliers and your
ear to the ground. Occasionally, if one of the fellows who worked at the
store was away on an errand, I may have given bum advice, but mostly
I was reliable, and had learned in a pinch to call on the old guys who sat
chewing the fat outside the store. Men didn't mind it was a woman
managing the best hardware in town, because I wasn't what the old-
timers still termed "a looker" and never was. Because I was finally the
age I was, for the first time in my life my chunky body seemed right.
Even my watermelon breasts kind of blended into my general mass
under a good old MacGregor plaid shirt that had been my favorite for
years.

I had been known to fix some things. If a fitting nut took to leak-
ing, such as the one under our old free-standing sink in the bathroom,
I could shut off the water and re-pack the nut with thread. I could wire
a light fixture, repair a toaster, and make a slow boy smile when he
came on Mondays after school. At the kitchen table I read to John and
taught him to use sentences to tell about what I was reading, taught
him words that came so hard to his tongue. I could bake a mean pie, as
the fellows at the store said, and I was calm when a customer came in
bothered by his project that was going wrong, the cause a piece we
didn't sell him, or maybe his own ignorance. But even before the time
of Kelly's fit, or seizure, which was what Ginger Dawn called it, I could
not fix what was going on between her and me.

At the start of Kelly's stay in our house, they nested as if they were
an old married couple on pillows on the veranda, smoking and watching the world go by. In the evenings they watched the old T.V., side by
side on the couch. In the mornings they politely took turns in the

bathroom. Down at the store they were saying, Saw that Mangiardi feller in the bar last night or on the street or over town. Said you stole his boy. But I never saw or heard from Morris Mangiardi, he didn't bother even to phone. Before Kelly came to us, he had stopped paying the pharmacy for Kelly's medication refills, which is why the boy had had the fit in our kitchen in the first place.

Because Kelly wasn't going to school, he was home on my weekday off and began to turn his hand to a few chores. He had no natural talent, that I could tell, at anything. He wasn't a mechanic or a plumber, wirer, or even an adequate dish washer, but he began to always be there, ready to pitch in, his eyes following me, flattering me with their attention. After a while Ginger Dawn began to treat me like the chief cook and bottle washer. She didn't help in the kitchen as she had always done, she no longer hung the clothes out on the line before school. Kelly and I gradually took over her jobs and by the middle of the third week, the two of us were often playing cribbage when she came home, comfortably settled in the kitchen, the bottle of whiskey and carton of skim milk between us, because we found we both enjoyed a little whiskey in our milk. This was on my day off, after John left. Towards the little fellow, Kelly behaved as you'd hope a big brother would. He'd help him pull off his jacket, push his chair closer to the table, ask him what his teacher'd said at school that day. And all the while, as the days went by, Kelly was watching me, but in what I came to see was a friendly, easy way. I stopped worrying about what he was seeing.

I had spent so much of my life marching forward, not once glancing back, that this whole section of it was like a segment from an orange that was to turn out bitter. You greedily swallowed, forgetting to chew, and the slice came sliding back up. Somewhere in that time I noticed that things began to cool between Ginger Dawn and the boy, who I suspected was lazy, deep-down, so it was just as well. I taught him how to mend and clear and stake the berry canes and he would do it, if I was there. But he always had to be told. Waiting to be told, he would sit in front of the T.V. mornings and on some afternoons he would go to the games arcade and play away the dollars I gave him for helping. He kept his hair slicked and his boots shined and he showered longer than any girl had time for. But Ginger Dawn was no longer charmed. Love, in her case, was not blind. One morning she shouted, "Geez, be responsible for your crap!" and went so far as to slam the door to the bathroom that he had left a mess. That sound of her screeching was not enough to actually shatter glass, but some invisible thing did break in our house and the next I knew she was packing.

It was after a simple supper of ham hock and lima beans that Kelly missed, because he was off somewhere without telling me. My nose was out of joint because when you went to the trouble to cook for somebody, they should be on time. There were some rules you had to let go of as kids grew up, but being home at suppertime was not one of them. Ginger Dawn always respected that, even if it meant coming home from pom-pom girl practice and going back again. That night we didn't talk at the table. I served Kelly's bowl and homemade bread on a plate beside it, as though he were going to sashay in the door any minute. "You are just sick," Ginger Dawn said and went to tucking it in. I was warming my bones sipping whiskey and milk and didn't pay her much attention. It had been a hard day at the store. The truck broke down near Gilmore loaded with the paint I'd promised City Hall, so they had the crew on the clock and no paint. I didn't heed Ginger Dawn when she first spoke, because her mouth had been coming on strong for a couple of weeks. Stiff-faced, she said, "You are sick," again. In her eyes was nothing you could call warm, but I felt from her an electricity that roused my arm hairs to attention. "You're a sicko drinker," she said. Although my arm hairs caught on, my mind didn't.

There may be moments in the scheme of a life where junctures appear in the heavens before you have the wits to figure out you're at one. A road gets taken that you're not even aware of in the passing instant, and whatever happens afterwards is too late to change. I didn't grasp this at the time. Instead, I bristled to something I sensed in the air. I bristled and I said, "I know what you are, I know what you are." But of course I didn't know who she was, I had lost track of her. What I meant, and it must have shown on my face, was what had been going on between Kelly and her, the sex. I was remembering the time he placed his jacket on the planks for her, as though he had done it before; I was remembering in the hallway when I caught him thrusting his tongue into her mouth; I was remembering bouts of muffled giggling late at night. I was burning with remembering the two of them together and I ached to strike out at her, Have you got a disease, are you pregnant. But I didn't speak, so distant in my past had the act of sex been, that it was taboo on my tongue. I felt naive as any virgin but more sheltered than some.

"You are disgusting," she said, huffing to her feet.

I was thinking of calling her a bitch, but I had never used the word. Imagining actually saying it moved me to throw my head back and laugh, and that's when her expression sucked in on itself. She turned and galloped up the stairs, leaving me stunned and muzzy-headed, my foolish, ill-timed laughter raucousing around the kitchen. The lima beans and ham in Kelly's bowl and in mine were congealing at a rapid pace. I cook hearty foods, full of natural fat, to help a body through lean times. Ginger Dawn wisely ate all hers.

In her bedroom, I sat on her pretty pink cotton chenille spread and blinked, trying to clear my head. "Come on," I whined, "come on, don't be silly, pretty please," but she just glared in my direction with her snake eyes and went on throwing skirts and sweaters into her duffel. She was intending to stay with a girlfriend who already had her own space in a rooming house and then they were going to get a place together, when Ginger Dawn found a job after school. Obviously she had plotted it already, which meant that for some time she'd been waiting for the right moment, the excuse to leave. I could not find the energy to take her on; she had got the jump on me and was so far around the track I would never catch up. Sitting on the bed, my shoulders hunched and my hands dangling between my knees, I thought of crazy things, I thought of phoning the police, I thought of knocking her out with a doll lamp I had given her for Christmas when she was five. The doll was a Southern belle, with a parasol and a wide-skirted blue dress and painted blue eyes that merrily watched our lives together coming undone by each thing my girl methodically packed. I thought of breaking that lamp to bits by knocking her out with it and then phoning the hospital. I thought of us in the ambulance. I thought of Ginger Dawn smelling of peaches, her arms around my neck. I thought of her saying she was sorry.

She galloped down the stairs two at a time and shut the door behind her quietly, which was unnerving, because it meant she was past the point of slamming. I sat on the foot of her neatly made twin bed, alone in her room, the twilight through the window that she left open because she preferred cold air while she slept. She always snuggled in her quilts, just her nose visible, and was more like a heap piled on the bed than a person lying in it. I used to tease her. I used to tease her about a lot of things. Her height, her stubbornness, the way when as a little girl concentrating on homework, her tongue stuck out the corner of her mouth.

I brought the bottle up and sat in the room in the Bentwood rocker and let the April coolness seep into me. I knew her going was not a tantrum. When Ginger Dawn did something, she did it all the way. I hated that boy and wanted him out of the house.

Spring is supposed to be the time of new beginning, but after Ginger Dawn moved out I felt like a corn stalk in a fall garden, still rooted but withering and losing my hold on the soil. Like the fun had gone and it would feel good to finally be uprooted and laid down once and for all and let the snow, so peacefully cold, pile up on the husk of what I once was. She moved the rest of her things out of the house while I was at work. I would come home and more stuff would be gone, her room barer and barer as though she were becoming invisible in pieces. I thought the way to behave was quietly, not to create a ruckus, not to try to shout her back. I thought it was a lark she was on, something a kid goes through, like when they begin to play house and boss all their babies around using your voice. I marked off the days and waited for her to come home. The longer I didn't do anything, the harder it was to think of what to do. I got so I couldn't choose one wrench over another or decide what to eat for lunch and I couldn't ask Kelly to leave, either.

Ginger Dawn was a minor and I could have gone to the police to get her back, but the one time I started out, I felt sick inside, like showing your dirty underpants to strangers. I knew she was still in school and doing all right. She had a job at the Crosstown Grocery. She was fifteen and three-quarters and acting, from what people said, like a sensible grown woman. I guessed you could have done worse as a result of bringing up a child. I needed the "three-quarters" business about her age. When people asked me, as they did at the bank or at the store, I sometimes said she was sixteen. Sometimes I couldn't stand thinking otherwise. It was too much like my child had died young.

I had come to a bad pass, I think a pioneer might say after travelling for a lifetime through the mountains only to find a crevasse or some other thing impossible to get across. I got to the point with whiskey that it was whiskey and me and on nights Kelly was out, which was more and more often, I talked to the bottle like some old women talk to cats. When you see yourself slumped over the kitchen table, your hands holding up your head, and you hear yourself telling a pitiful joke to a bottle and then watch yourself splash a bit into the bottom of your empty glass, just one splash more as a nightcap that lasts, some nights, til near dawn, that's when you become afraid in a more general way and feel as helpless as an infant must, left in its crib too long, when it finds itself alone, beyond the hunger that made it cry out in the first place.

Kelly was like those men you read about who miss a dinner one night and come in late the next, and then on the third, on his way in, might bring you flowers picked from the wild ones growing alongside the shed. He drank my whiskey and sometimes we played cribbage. Then after supper, often he was gone again and I was left doing needlepoint, which I am not good at and don't like, in front of the T.V. by myself.

On a Monday, on one of my days off, annoyed at Kelly because he wasn't home and we were supposed to clean out cupboards, I started drinking after a lunch of crackers and some cheese that was going moldy. It was going moldy because I never got around to fixing my macaroni and cheese dish for Kelly. It was his favorite, served with lots of fresh pepper ground on top, and he liked to eat it with a spoon. I wasn't going to fix the dish because Kelly might not come home to eat it and I would be left waiting at the table like a spinster, her face all scrubbed and shiny, one of those sad stories, a flower in her hair and the candles lit. I fell asleep in the afternoon, lying on the couch and dead to the world, so dead, in fact, that I forgot it was story day. When I came to, it was twilight and on the veranda steps sat John, his head cradled in his spindly arms, resting on his knees. I looked at the clock on the mantle. He would have been there over two hours.

"Are you sick?" he asked when he saw me in the doorway, my hair no doubt mussed. He scrambled to his feet and squeezed his arms around as much of my hips as they would go. I felt nothing, not even the disgust at myself I knew I ought to. I told him I had the flu. I told him to go on home.

At almost two in the morning I heard Kelly downstairs, crashing around, bumping into things. A glass broke, or what sounded like a glass, and I reached over and turned on my lamp, which scooted off the night table and landed on the rug, unbroken, its pink shade bent and blaring light at the ceiling. I opened my mouth and croaked at Kelly, and then my throat freed, I was so suddenly mad, and sounds went baying forth, like something a hound dog might come up with in a fit of temper. I struggled to get out of bed but was held fast, wrapped in sweaty sheets and my comforter. I struggled, and all the while my belly was giving rise to noise that worked its way along my throat and into my mouth that felt full to bursting. I wanted this stranger out of my house. I wanted him gone.

"Jesus God!" Kelly said, stumbling on the stairs. "Will you give it a rest. They'll think I'm killing you over here."

While he was making his way up, I wrestled to get free and slid onto the floor head and shoulders first, like a newborn baby out of its mother, except I was already wearing swaddling clothes. My feet and legs and the skirt part of my nightgown were tangled in the sheets. When he opened my door like he owned the place and saw me, I wanted to faint from the humiliation. But fainting wouldn't have been enough. What I needed was simple, straightforward dying.

He started across, and I could see, my neck twisted and upside down as it was, how his spurs snagged on my new plum-colored rug. "Don't wear those spurs in the house," I bawled.

"You're not my mother," he flung back, but the words that themselves sounded angry didn't keep him from bending over me. "Here," he said and pulled on the sheets and eased my legs out of the snarl they were in. His hands were warm and his long shapely fingers looked so pretty by lamplight that when he reached, I let him touch a tit through my nightgown.

For a change he wasn't watching me, he was squatting beside me watching his own hand quivering on what must have been the biggest one he'd ever touched. The nipple stiffened and roughened itself against the nightgown. I felt the heat from his fingers as he tugged at that eager nipple and then he moved and lay on the carpet facing me, propped on an elbow, and shut his eyes and groaned. I was staring at that pretty man's hand on a part of me that had not been touched in so long, and I was swooning, the feeling of it oozing like syrup all through me, my eyes almost rolling in my head like a baby feeding. And when he took his hand away, I reached for it back. My reach was more like a grab.

I knew the look that crossed his face then, though it was difficult to focus my eyes. I knew because it was the mingling of disgust and pity my own young face used to get on it. There was fear, too, in Kelly's thin features, because he was trapped. I have seen that fear in a dog's eyes when its master comes at it batting a newspaper for something it did or did not do. Being trapped causes a dog to be cowardly and a man, too. And then, like any creature snagged, Kelly began weighing his choices, his brain behind bloodshot eyes clicking away like a calculator. He was deciding how far to go and what he might get in the long run that had nothing much to do with pleasure. In that way he was already a whore, one of those men who live in expensive resorts and wait for lonely rich women to come along. A gigolo. Of course he didn't desire me. No one had ever desired me, in the way you read about in the romance books or even in the simple way you hear about in marriage.

The curl dropped over his forehead as he lay beside me on my new rug. He didn't brush the curl back, of course, because it looked appealing and boyish, and drunk as he was, he was aware of himself and how to get by. His long-lashed eyes filled with tears.

"Please," I said then. "Please." I heard myself saying those words.

He shifted away so his back was to me and pulled his knees toward his chest and put his hands between them. Curled in that fetal position, he looked like the child he deeply was. My face felt slapped, hard, the way in winter, wind and bitter cold tearing your eyes causes the skin on your cheeks to grow thick and stiff like hide. Inside your clothes, if you are dressed right, your body heat stokes up and fills your woolen underwear and down jacket that smells of truck oil. The heat of your body pours through you while your eyes do their watering, and that was how it was with me lying smashed and shameless on the floor. The coldness left me and I was burning, my whole body blushing and hurting and at the same time bereft, because it had not been touched; nor should it have been, I know, by that boy no older than a son if I had thought to have one.

"No," he said, rolling back. I wished he hadn't spoken. His voice was husky and theatrical-sounding and he still had the tears clinging to his lashes as he looked at me. Then he reached his hand to touch my tit again. The tip of his tongue flicked between his parted lips, small flicks that made his tongue look tiny and not the grown size it certainly was. His lips were puffy and reddened, as though he had used them well already. He tore his eyes away from his hand on my tit and rested them on mine. His tongue went on moving. His shoulders made cuddling gestures, as though he would like to nestle close. He watched me.

The room was whirling around and I deliberately, slowly rotated my eyes in their sockets to feel the hardness of them, the sockets, and the pull of the muscles holding them in place. I did that because I was, I knew, very drunk and unable to rescue myself. Feeling the bones of my eye sockets reminded me of skulls you see in science classes and being reminded was a way of forgetting what the boy had said and what he had not done. Thinking of my skull down in the ground, cleaned by worms and bugs, was a way of trying to escape from shame that had followed me my whole life through and wasn't done with me yet. My nightgown, the pull-down kind that had a loose elastic at its rounded neck, had flowers on it, blue rosy-looking faded English flowers. The pink background had weakened to almost white and the cloth was thin. Through the pilled, often-washed cotton my breasts were soft balloons, the nipples dark knobs and looking like the part of a balloon you blow into. I did what it seemed I was meant to do and went through with it. I shifted to a more comfortable position and pulled down the elastic on my nightgown and reached in and I gave him one.

There is no fool like an old fool is what they say, and I was experiencing it firsthand. In the morning I had a hangover which I wished was worse than it was, my memory might then have been sidetracked. I lay in bed a long time but did not feel at home. Kelly slept late and came downstairs near noon and sat at the table tapping his pretty fingers on the cloth and grinning while I fried the bacon and eggs, and chopped onions for the hashbrowns the way he liked them and didn't know why I did that, either. He acted as though nothing had happened but I knew something had happened, the way when you're watching someone talking at a podium and maybe staring too hard at them, trying to understand their words, the world tilts, or jumps, to the right or to the left, shifts anyway and it doesn't matter any more what that person is saying, about whether the government is going to subsidize the farmers more or less this year, because something has shifted. That's the way it was that morning. The boy sat there grinning like a creature licking his chops. And I was the prey, already snared. He didn't have to watch me so closely as before. This I noticed while cooking, he just took up humming and gazing out the window onto the rows of raspberries and acted like a man who had a sure thing, a pig in the poke, no hunger this winter. I put his plate down in front of him and he kept on smiling, but to himself, not at me. Like my da used to do.

You could have knocked me over. I stumbled with that thought, reeling back, as I have read of people doing when something hidden comes as clear to them as bones found bleached by a desert sun. It was hot where I went in that moment. The reeling back, that loss of footing, did happen to me, but the only witness to it wrapped his arm closer around his plate as though I were simply staggering and might fall into his food and spoil it.

＊

On the mornings of a spraying day the plane from Connell Field would drone overhead like a pregnant bee. It was a crop duster, full of poison like I had come to realize Kelly was, and heading to the big farms further south. Sometimes I used to wonder about the pilot of that plane, what he was thinking, for I knew it would a man who was flying. In the evenings I used to sit on the veranda and sometimes see the plane return, and wonder at the pilot's mood, at what dials he was looking at, or if he suspected anybody on their veranda, glass of comfort by their side, watching him in his machine. Sometimes at the end of the day he would lark in the air, dive and catch himself like kids do the ball when they're playing jacks.

Following me now along the switch-backs of the Oregon coast was a small plane, a high-winged one, flying low, bouncing in the wind so that the pilot had to be feeling like a lone pea in a tin can. The sound of his engine was company, and I was grateful because of the hard time I was having, fighting off a sense of danger. Wind was battering the truck and the dark clouds over the ocean looked like heavy rain. But what alarmed me more was me. I was trembly deep down, like the earth before it comes up with some disaster. My body was slowly falling into a fit of some kind. I was dizzy behind my eyes, and that dizziness was what a seizure must be like, except so far I hadn't lost consciousness or got to the frothing stage. My fingers stayed clenched on the wheel and my eyes kept on driving. It was an uneasiness I had, an earthquake overtaking me from the inside, with the power to sweep the truck off this wind-blown stretch, over the guard rail that flowed along the snaky roadway like a live and peaceful creature. I saw the truck slammed onto the dripping dark boulders near the shore, where I would be killed and not able to say my piece to my da. My brain would go out all brown from stewing in its own juice.

I tried muttering to myself. I tried humming a little tune. But the quaking didn't stop. My hands turned the wheel to the left, to the right, following the deserted road like they knew it. I spoke to the pilot in the plane overhead. I said, "Hey. Whiskey must've soaked right through my brain. Hey, maybe it's a screw come loose." Thinking I was lucky to have lasted so long.

Hearing my own voice trying to talk to itself, or to me, or to both of us, disturbed me further. The voice didn't sound like mine. Which isn't right. It did sound like mine, but the hearing of it in the cab of my truck on that twisty highway going where I didn't know, had separated my voice and me from ourselves, and the one was startled to hear the other. From the sudden recklessness of my driving that happened during this idea, I figured I ought to pull over rather than be thrown into the sea. Because likely I would not plunge cleanly into the water and die instantly, but instead would dent the guard rail, wreck up the truck and in general cause a great deal of worry for myself and whoever came along for the rescue, if anybody ever would. The situation could prove to be a damn nuisance, as my mother used to say about the details in life, which as far as I could tell were just about everything there was.

The body that used to be mine would be carted somewhere dark to be studied for its non-stop trembling that had no physical cause that could be found. They would take notice of the body's disembodied voice and its eyes bugging out and its heart shattering itself inside its case, like a box of Christmas ornaments, your most precious ones that you drop from the ladder you are balanced on to get near the top of a too-tall tree that you drove miles and miles to find in woods that were illegal, in the first place, to cut from. And you go ahead and cut a tree anyway and haul it home in the back of the truck under all the tarp and canvas you could find when you set out, so that you can please your daughter, who is seven and missing the man she thinks is her da, who is dead. For lots of things you feel guilty. You drop the box of your favorite ornaments while wobbling on the ladder, due to a hangover, which turns out to be only a first of many. As the box nears the floor, your eyes catch it in slow motion. It tilts and picks up speed, does a dive and smashes all it holds, including Ginger Dawn's favorite, a fragile pink Christmas tree ball with Baby Jesus and a lamb set inside, for which you suspect she has never truly forgiven you.

I swerved over into what maybe was someone's private road or maybe a county one, off 101 anyway, and into some trees. My brain had obviously begun bubbling and boiling while my body was shaking and my teeth clamping. I had a frozen moment where I thought I was dying. The sickness would be some virus or other as yet undetected by medical science and powerful enough to kill me right there, and the thought of actually dying scared me to death. For what was a long time but probably shorter than it felt, I bawled. I rolled on the fake-fur covered seat of my truck and onto the floor, as much of me as could fit there, and back again, clawing at the windows and at my face and I even pulled on my hair, something you generally only read about in books.

When my senses came back, the plane was long gone, which was just as well. For a while I had been worrying about the pilot, thinking it would be worse to be lost in the sky than on the ground. But even being able to pull off and stop, the fact was it was me who was lost. I had become a person who for sixteen years had not been more than 100 miles from my own house. Since Ginger Dawn was born until lately I had never been without her for more than a child's sleep-over that I could recall. And yet I had been so foolish as to think I could just hop in the truck and drive the nine hundred miles and some to Ukiah, CA, which is where I last heard from my da years ago, just drive out of town as casually as delivering the jam to Schofield or Tyler.

After a while I inched back out onto the road, preparing myself for the whacking of the wind, and drove steady with my jaws clenched and my eyes almost afraid to blink. I turned into the first motel I found and paid for two nights. It was a Travelodge and the price was steep. I might have landed something more reasonable had I been able to look, but I was past being able. I paid and I holed up with what was left of my fifth and I ate in their coffee shop twice a day and hung out in between, sipping the watery brew they made, so the old girls waitressing there recognized me and in the way of employees in places where travellers pass through, they took to acting as though they knew me. And the feeling I got felt a bit like home and I began to calm down.

All in all I tracked my da a month, through May, on the road and having my talks with him. I pictured tearful scenes and him saying he was sorry and meaning it. I dreamt of him and pieces of our early life, the details of which I forgot as soon as my eyes opened. In one dream that was a nightmare, a body I figured was his blew up from festering pestilence and exploded all over everything. One of those dreams in which you think you are a happy dreamer until you look down and see the slime all over yourself, because all along you were the one standing too close.

I drank some and on occasion had to stay put, but generally I felt fine. Summer was coming on but not yet and I was alone on the beaches running in and out of the cold and wild surf, a few sea gulls and those long-legged high-strung shore birds and me. But then I would drive and think some more. I was sorry about a lot of things, I was sorry I had not let Ginger Dawn get a cat, which I was allergic to, or a dog which I wasn't. When she was little and wanted a dog I couldn't get myself to see it through and by the time I was clearer, she was into wanting a horse. I could have used a dog about now. His name would be Bowser and he would be the color of a baked potato skin. He would be sitting proud, looking out the windshield just like a normal person, filling the passenger seat with his smelly presence and whining now and again, for the sake of conversation.

While driving or in the cheap motels or while camping on my Army cot in some hidden off-the-road spot, I thought about my mother too and the little card I had once received from her sister, during the time I was cooking for a small sheep outfit in Montana. The card, with forget-me-nots watercolored onto it by hand, was mailed from a city back east with no return address. Writing but making sure nobody could write back, or moving and forgetting to tell anybody was my family's way of keeping shut of each other and it worked. The card said that my mother and her new husband had died in a car crash outside of Baton Rouge, a place I had only heard of and knew nothing about. Baton Rouge always sounded, if you say it right and I do because I looked it up, like the kind of place that would smell of wisteria and lilacs year round. For all my travels by bus I never went there, because I forgot to, in the way you do memories and people left far behind.

On the trail of my da it didn't do any good to think about my mother who was tall, on the scale of Ginger Dawn, but built sturdy, more like me, and not nearly as graceful as the granddaughter she missed by walking out on me when I was fourteen. She left me and my da behind to do for each other, as her note tucked under the plastic doily on my dresser said. I didn't know what she meant by "do for each other"; I didn't know if she meant all that she might have or even if she knew what my da was up to. Because like Ginger Dawn who must have inherited it from her, when my mother made her mind up, she went whole hog. I never heard from her after she left, not so much as a birthday card. She never did much like me.

Ukiah, the town I headed for first, was on the brink of getting too big. It was tucked inland along a stretch of 101 that straightened out in a businesslike fashion, more like a road you could use to make a dash down to San Francisco on, while wearing a suit and tie.

There I found my da's old rooming house with Bettey Forbert still running it. At the time he moved away, he had lost his job, she said, but she didn't know whether he was fired or quit on his own. Some things, she said, were men's affairs and she wasn't much on details, but she did confess to being a one for love. "He's been gone three years, but I pine for him still," she said while I feasted by myself on her home-baked tea breads and cakes. She started batting her eyelashes and I saw that they were false ones she was wearing, dabbed with blue mascara. She resembled what Ginger Dawn's spider-eyed roommate would be doing to herself forty years into the future.

The fact was, Bettey Forbert's house was a lot like the rooming house Ginger Dawn was in back home. Both houses were in old parts of town, on quiet side streets. This one had a single rose bush under a living room window and some scraggly ice plant and some weed clumps for lawn, just the sort of taste in landscaping my da had. Ginger Dawn's place, when I saw her before I left, had a box elder out front and although the yard was littered with soggy candy wrappers and odds and ends that had been hiding under the snow all winter, the inside turned out to be clean enough. The landlady was thin and unsmiling, but I did not mind, since it was not her I had come to see.

Bettey Forbert poured more coffee and I thought she was going to talk about my da, but it was soon apparent she was telling about soaps, the stories, and getting those people confused with her "friends", she called them, the roomers who had stayed in her place over the years. I sat back, content to rest in somebody's soft, real-home sofa with doilies pinned carefully on its back and arms, and let myself think of my girl. Ginger Dawn hadn't given me much of a welcome when I went to visit. She opened the door a hand's width and looked at me with a routine smile on her face while behind her, drawers that sounded stuck or old were being jiggled shut. I figured a tidying-up was going on and that if a child still carried you inside, even as her conscience, then you were connected despite the smile that was not a bit personal, just one of those making her lips stretch.

Her roommate was a girl named Sally who worked full time at the Sears. She was chubby and had too much black goop on her eyes, but she shook my hand politely and excused herself so Ginger Dawn and I could be alone. She was one of six and from a farm outside of town, Ginger Dawn said, and she saw her family every Sunday. Maybe she wanted to rub it in that she herself had not come home once, in the month since she had moved, except to lug things off when I wasn't around. We were strangers sitting on the two straight chairs they had in that room and like strangers we chatted, teeth and lips and vocal boxes doing a familiar exercise and our eyes looking over each other's heads or staring at our feet while fingers picked at cloth on our knees or those pill-like things on our sweaters.

Finally I handed her a check and watched her face try not to be surprised at the size of it. I told her she could move back into the house. Kelly was gone, and I had already talked to the owners of the store, who lived in Willamette, and they had made one of the long-time fellows an interim manager. I was giving her a gift, but I wanted something from her, I knew I did.

I became aware then that Bettey Forbert had wound down and was watching me. I sighed and tried a smile and ate another slice of her still-warm tea bread and glanced at the room, which was plain as the outside with its one rose bush, everything was plain, including the rest of Bettey Forbert's face with no make-up on it, not even a hint of lipstick or a pat of powder or a smudge of blush on her sallow cheeks. She just had those big eyes that called attention to themselves, like Yoo Hoo-ing from one farm to the next. That loud. She said, "Your dad ate just the same. Such enthusiasm it was heartwarming," and then she smiled, with something wan and wispy about it, and invited me to stay for supper. That's when I felt the noose start to tighten around my neck, as it must have done for my da, with this good woman not eating and watching your every move and maybe depending on it to keep her going.

Over the next week, on Bettey Forbert's advice, I backtracked all the way to Trinidad, north of Eureka. It took finding two other rooming houses and a derelict hotel, phoning the Humboldt County Social Services and showing up in person at the Eureka police station before I located his whereabouts, in Redwoods Hospital. His trail zigzagged like a night snail that in the morning you can see has doubled back on itself more than once, for reasons only it knows.

The night before I went to visit him at the hospital, I stayed in the motel room to celebrate, a cheap one that smelled of needing new paint and of lino that wasn't rinsed clean, because my money was already starting to run out. I was drinking from two smelly glasses at once. They were plastic glasses, with ridges on the outside so a hand could get a grip on them, and they smelled of old soap ground into their scratches. They had the look of an old glass I found while digging in the squash garden, Ginger Dawn by my side, the remains of a garbage burial left by pioneers who lived on our land before us. But these glasses were lightweights and made a hollow sound when you bonked them together empty and a not much better sound when you thonked them together full. Which I was doing a lot of. They were so light it was easy to drink quite a bit because it felt like nothing. I drank from one and then I toasted my da and drank from the other. I drank to the da I had hunted down like one of those fox dogs do, running without quitting, you would've had to kill it first. And I was going to have my say, get a load off my mind, a weight off my chest and speak all those things you do when you are madder than a wet hen, mad as all get out, cross as a bear and breathing fire and fury. Get out I told him once and he did. He left, all right, he was a timid fellow who would obey you if he was cowed enough. He left from Bill's place and I had not seen him since, although he did write from Bettey Forbert's. But he never really left me, and in this case I saw it was not his fault. It was me keeping him. Now I was ready to be done with him, I was seeing it all like a visionary on a mountain that you read about who can levitate themselves with just their minds, taking their body and all. I was ready to be done with him and fly.

"To you, Da," I toasted, bowing to the blank T.V. screen. I was talking to the screen, practicing my speeches one last time. I accused him of perfidy and other big words that I wasn't entirely sure the meaning of, but they sounded good coming off my tongue. I accused him of child abuse, that I had read about in a magazine. I hadn't known there was such a state, of being abused I mean, hadn't known it enough to put words to it. And when first I read about it and realized how popular it was, I thought the crying that burst out of me would be enough, but it wasn't. You hold on and I don't know why. To the screen I said, "Bad bad bad!" to him, sounding like a child, maybe aged ten and some. Which made my knees want to buckle, because I was that old when he first came to my room.

I tried to toast myself and my new life, whatever it was, but I was snivelling by then. I made a long distance call to the house, but Ginger Dawn was not there and I suspected that in her own stubborn way she still had not moved back and never would. Then I put the phone down and took the glasses, one in each hand, and finished them off and bruised my leg on the edge of the coffee table when I fell over it and onto the sofa. It had a smell too, of dogs and other odors I didn't want to think about.

The hospital was a two-storey wood building, probably built with redwood because there was a stump out front with a plaque of some kind nailed to it. It was an old hospital and there was a backhoe parked next to a dug foundation and footings in place, for what looked like an additional wing, and some steel beams and concrete blocks in piles. It seemed like an abandoned job, rain tarps strewn where wind must have blown them, and nobody at work, which was just as well. My head was not in a favorable mood for loud noise.

The nurse at the second floor station was surprised to see me, because she said they hadn't thought my da had any living relatives. She was an Irish girl from the sound of her and when she heard herself coming close to scolding me, she colored from her neck to her cheeks. As our steps echoed down the corridor to my da's room, my heart was meanwhile pounding clear into my head. In one breath, the nurse said that he was in a two-bed room and that I was not to be shocked by his appearance. But I wasn't listening. Not well enough, anyway, because I was. Shocked. What I saw was my da unconscious, looking something like a mummy would if it was unwrapped. He was hooked up to machines that, while I stared, beeped and sighed and slurped at his body juices, recycling them, putting some in and taking some out again.

His head was shaved and a baseball-sized swelling on the left side of it welled out purple and red, little whiskery things growing all over his skull. He looked dead, the color you always think of as dead, kind of sad yellow. He was like a wax museum character some cruel person had attached to the throat gurglers, for a joke on Halloween night. In that baseball-sized swelling was where the blood or fluids, the nurse said, were gathering, and I figured, to burst inward into his brain when the skin of his skull could stretch no more. My da's bruise recalled Kelly's face when his own da bashed him, and I didn't know if there ever was an end to parents doing wrong by their children.

The nurse slid a chair under me and I put my arms on the thin metal supports of the chair and I sat there like Abraham Lincoln in that place he sits, my face wearing his thoughtful frown, my feet planted. Finally I said I didn't know why they bothered, keeping him alive is what I meant, but the little nurse said the hospital wasn't real busy just then, they had the bed available. Then she pulled back and because she was fair-skinned Irish, turned red again. "What I mean is, you never know, do you now? There's always hope he'll be coming round unexpected and be asking for his porridge bright as day." She poured on the cheerful business, but even she couldn't keep on, because the fact was we were right beside his bed, and it was obvious nothing lying in that bed looked like any amount of hope had a chance.

I was not prepared for the sorry case he had become and I had to choke back tears and more than tears. I had to choke back bile, because he had cheated me again. The nurse explained that there was bleeding in his skull and that was what one tube was for, draining everything but brains. She didn't put it that way, but the point was, she wanted it clear that my da, his mind, was not home. One glance and I had known that this shell of a man could not fondle his little girl's tit while he did his business pushing against her side, nor could his lips suck on it and make her feel ashamed because it felt good. And all the ranting I had rehearsed myself for, all the speeches I made up while driving south, the bottles I downed for courage, would be wasted because my da had slimed off, like the snail I had thought about earlier. He had slimed off, is what it came to, and just left his body behind.

The fellow in the other bed wouldn't talk when I went over to introduce myself after supper. He stared at me with blue eyes that had a person behind them but not revealing anything. He had white hair spiking out all over his head and his cheeks were thin, with a single furrow running down each one.

They had my da shaved, but not thorough. The nurse who came on in the evening, so young she was thin as a sliver and had hair chopped by what looked like a chain saw, told me they would have spruced him up a bit had they known I was coming but now it didn't matter since I had already seen him. She said it was hard enough to be in the hospital and smell it, without your own father looking like a rummy. That was her word, rummy. Then she pulled her mouth down like she'd said something, but you knew she didn't really think so. She was young and the young, in my experience with Ginger Dawn, went out of their way to speak their minds.

Overall, when I squinted my eyes, my da was sprouting tubes like a rotten potato left in a dark cellar. It was tough to be as old as I was and feel that young when I looked at him. Knees weak. Stomach about to give out. Words gone from my mind and along with it, the memory of ever having had any in the first place.

I was thinking of pulling the chair closer to the bed, trying to act natural, when I heard, behind the curtain of my da's neighbor, voices talking. A visitor must have arrived when I was in the can down the hall. "She's hard," a woman's voice said, "she don't have a bit of female softness about her." And the old fellow replied, "She's never been married, I would raise you five on that. Something secret about her, something bad. Ugly, too. Ugly as a dog." "A pity, I do declare," the woman went on and if she said any more, I missed it because I turned on tiptoes and left. I didn't want to embarrass them. That's what I thought, anyway, ordering a double at the first bar I came to.

The next day I didn't go in, but after that acted like a hospital old-timer. I managed to close down my nose and ignore the sour-clothes smell of bodies in bed too long, and I didn't pay attention to the general Lysol-scented decay in the building itself. Wood tended to take on the smells of the life it sheltered, and an old hospital was no exception. I would come in, nod at the nurse at the desk or at the cook's helper wheeling trays of food to folks who would complain about it, but not giving any to my da because he wouldn't know the difference, being beyond the bitterness of potato flakes. All I could figure, it must have been the preservatives, or else some fake butter they were mashed with to reduce cholesterol, as if anybody on the second floor would care, so ancient most of them, they must have been praying to be gone from this veil of tears, those that had any sense left at all. I was to spend days in an orange vinyl chair beside my da's bed, staring at his remains and watching his chest jerk up, sink down with the accordion breather clicking at his side.

I avoided regular visiting hours, hoping my da's unfriendly room-mate would not be having that visitor. I had learned to enter the room, making a cheery greeting. "Good day, Da, and how are you doing?" I chirped, loud, like one of the nurses, who acted as though they expected any minute he would pull the tubes out of his nose and mouth and give a greeting back.

After a week of my routine, my da began to look like someone I had known. Not that he had changed, at a glance he resembled any other down-and-outer, but the fact was, now I could see him, compare how he was with how he used to be. And I understood it was me who knew him in a way nobody else did. Occasionally there was something senti-mental in how I looked upon him, depending partly on the quantity of whiskey I'd had before coming in; but it occurred to me that I had seen his face all my life, in sin and in sorrow, and that I was the only one alive who had witnessed this particular face and body when it was young and moved to its own spirit.

In a drawer I found a pad and pencil and calculated that even with missing time, I had been close-hand to my da off and on for twenty-five years of his life. Longer than I had known Ginger Dawn. Longer than I had known anybody, except pieces and glimmers of myself. The responsibility of witnessing made my belly shiver. But what was hap-pening inside my da was private, maybe always had been. What was going on between him and the machines had nothing to do with me. And who I was didn't make a difference to it.

I sat forward and peered at him. His eyes were slits with the eyeballs themselves sometimes moving up in his head like in exasperation or to the side as though to spy. They were milky blue and the whites weren't white but bloodshot and sulphur-colored. His eyelashes were almost gone, they never were much, pale as dandelion seed on the wind, and his skin, especially around the nose, was patchy with silvery scales. His lips were puffy, as anybody's would be with tubes stuck in them, and dry, scales there too and flickers of saliva in the corners of his mouth, crusted in creases that were red and sore-looking. He had stubble on parts of his face, the hollows of the cheeks where the nurses ran the razor by fast. His whole face when you squinted was greyish underneath but somehow a jolly shade on the surface of it, like you'd picture Santa Claus after a rum toddy or two.

His feet were poking out from under the lightweight lemon-colored blanket and I crept down to inspect them. They smelled of disinfectant and dying skin and had whorls on the balls for all the miles he had walked. There were left-over blister patches, too, and a bunion outside the right little toe that was unhealed and practically raw to the bone. It had a henna stain, as though a nurse had dabbed on Bactine. The bottoms of his toes were flat, and the nails looked like globs of dried dark gold wax like what you'd pull from the ears of an elephant if you could get near enough.

I raised my head and shook it, taking a deep breath. What I had been studying was, after all, just a body. It was helpless and shrunken. It never had been very big, as men's bodies go. It was hard to believe that this particular one and what had lived within it used to have the power to frighten me so.

Voices speaking, again, the same two, as I come to after a nap: "She ain't been to see her old man in more'n fifteen years." The second one, a woman's: "She looks the type, awright. Tough. One of them as favors females. You know."

Having dozed off in the chair, I was headachey and stiff and found my feet under the covers, against my da's cold shin bones. It seemed the old geezer in the next bed had that visitor again, the nosy one, who must have seen me asleep as she went by. The wall clock said I had been folded in the chair for almost an hour. I stretched and coughed and yawned, making big noisy ho-hums. But the voices went on. The old fellow said, "Oh. Probably never been married. Never wanted to, you mean." And the woman said, "You got my drift. It's unnatural, females like that. Plumb unnatural."

I turned beet red realizing who and then what they meant. How could the nasty things I thought they meant pop into my mind so fast if there wasn't some truth in it? But I had enough whiskey still in me from the morning that I pushed myself up and crept to the foot of my da's bed, ready for a fight. The beige curtain separating the two beds was attached by hooks to one of those horseshoe shaped tracks on the ceiling. I grabbed a wad of it in my fist and gave it a spin, kind of like they do on "Wheel of Fortune" on T.V., and then had to yank my way around to the end of it, anyway, because it jerked and fluttered more than actually moved. What I saw was the old geezer lying in his bed and he was all alone. He grinned when he saw me, opening his mouth wide, showing the gaps in his teeth. My da and him both without their teeth, the mouths of them gaping like caves, no barriers between me and their personal dark. I was a grown-up woman but felt afraid all over again. I whipped that curtain over my face and clung to it, hanging there for dear life. I was on a rollercoaster moving backwards through time, a trip that I guess I had asked to be on.

I drove to Trinidad and walked through a small woods to the shore, found some rocks and sat on one, staring out to sea. Nobody in my family really liked it, sex, from what I had pieced together, although my da went through the ritual. It was natural for a dirty-minded old man to think I was a Lesbian, I used to think so, too, after Leslie. For awhile, I hardly touched Ginger Dawn, worrying something from me would contaminate her. But when I didn't find myself following teenage girls around, I figured what happened was a random event, rather than the start of a new habit.

Except for Bill, who was old and a bachelor for reasons of his own, I never lived with a man and even then, we never touched each other. In my time I had had a man or two, if that's how you say it, "had". I think more likely I was the one had, especially the morning Ginger Dawn was conceived, in an alley in Cleveland, where a gang of young men dragged me. They were all colours which is why she is cinnamony, I liked to think, although I had read enough to know that such an idea is against human biology.

The circumstances of her conception were a shame I used to carry, but much later, I decided I was glad if that's what it took to get me my girl. Being so slow, by the time I would have got around to having a child naturally, I would have been past menopause and into the way-too-late of my life.

It happened before dawn on a day that turned out to be pretty if you were in the mood for a bright fall sun and the leaves turning crispy and falling from the trees. I had just come off the bus from Louisville and was looking for a cheap hotel to wash in. Bus stations where they were, in the dirtiest parts of downtowns that were deserted until the pawnshops and office buildings opened, I was a sitting duck. Safety never crossed my mind.

In my experience boys always found someone prettier to pick on, but these were not regular boys. It was four grabbed me but only three did their business in my body, I think, maybe because my thighs were slimy by their turn. In any event, I don't know for sure because I did what I had always done with my da. "Hold her down", I heard them say, but they didn't have to cut me with their knife and no one had to hold me. I already knew how to be still. I closed my eyes and shifted from my body to outside it, biding my time some place else, the sound of wings fluttering in my ears. Later I didn't think the sound was wings, although I concentrated hard on them at the time. Later I thought the racket was the brain part of me doing its best to keep separate from the rest.

What I had wanted from her, Ginger Dawn, when I left was a sadness so deep I would feel it forever. What I wanted was for her to cry out that I should not go, should not leave her. For her to need me so much that I would have to go through the trouble of unpacking the truck and fighting for my job back. But she was stubborn and wouldn't lie. She raised her eyes, met mine.

"Okay," I said and headed for the door.

Finally, she wept, acting like a girl who had a mother, but it was slow getting going. Her face, so pretty and creamy, so cocky around its mouth, began to dissolve, like a child's does, the bottom lip holding fast before stammering loose. She threw her arms around me and wept into my hair. Without half trying, I could still feel her hot tears soaking right down to my scalp and running into my ears.

But then, "Good luck, Mom," she said, and too bad for me, I'd thought at the time, I was free to go.

I lost the horizon and the ship I'd been noticing without much attention. It was my da's fault that had turned me so passive, that had, somehow, separated me from something important, that had mutated me into a dwarf of myself.

After two weeks at the hospital every day, watching him get nowhere, not sleeping much myself and burdened by hangovers too often, one afternoon I started talking. "I hate you, you old bastard," I said first, in a normal voice, my eyes glaring like you do at a child that's come to the end of your tether. It was quiet in the room for a minute, just my voice hovering there, sounding out of place alongside the respirator's rhythmic background noise that may as well have been real silence, I was so used to it. Then I heard a coughing from the window bed and felt a stab of ill will toward that other old man, toward his eavesdropping and basic deep-down meanness. My legs didn't give me a chance to consider, I stood and marched over to his side and meant to just put him in his place but once found, my voice didn't stop. "And you," I said, "you be quiet. I never did anything to you. All I ever did was be good and do what you wanted and all I wanted was for you to treat me nice." By the time I got to the first "you bastard", something in me realized I was spouting off to the wrong one. This one was grinning, his eyes alight by the excitement and he wasn't my da at all but that other fool.

"I hate you, you old bastard," I said, raising my voice, and I did, too. Hate him. It flared in me. His fingers groped for the call button and I turned away in a scuffle of bewilderment to look upon my da, machines rasping and tubes bubbling. There was nobody home. Only a crazy person would ask for love from a blind, brain-dead old man or, for that matter, from a stranger. But since I had the stage and they were cornered, the only thing I could do was keep on. "You!" I shouted, pointing to the face most resembling my da's when he was young and handsome in his way, "you!" I shouted, recalling as a child how I used to crawl onto his lap for comfort, while likely he was busy being distracted by his personal swelling, me being so close. "You are a filthy pig, you take it back." I swung toward the other geezer, my finger still pointing. This one had said I was nasty, different and odd; I remembered the times he said ugly things to me and touched my body but never saw me, never really me. "I hate you, I hate you, I hate you, I love you, oh daddy da," I cried to a strange old man now looking terrified in his bed, "you damn old bastard," and then in tears I spun on my heel as they do in old movies, those women in their full-length dresses, flounces on the skirts, their chins atop long necks held high, and in passing my da's bed, some bad words from Ginger Dawn's vocabulary ricocheted in my head and I bellowed, "You, too, turkey guts," and fled head-first into the closed door and knocked myself for a loop.

Sometimes in attempting to speak their piece, a person can find themselves in a prickly pickle, as was the case with me. The situation might have been embarrassing as all get out. The nurses, the Irish one and a bigger one more my age who I didn't recognize, scraped me off the floor and Bactined and bandaged my forehead. They were not gentle about it, either, because they had heard the ruckus my mouth was making, yelling as it was, upsetting patients and using cuss words besides, as the big one put it. But I was not worried by them; I figured that what you draw together in a hurry when you are at last hellbent on expressing yourself is probably just right. When they had me on my feet, I escaped from their clutches for a moment and slithered over to give a final snake-eyed stare to the geezer by the window; and it worked, he looked away. All in all it had been a complicated scene, and though it had its confusing moments, it was full of genuine thunder and tarnation.

✳

Sometimes you think the only entertainment people in a country town have is to check in the bushes to see who's doing what to who when they shouldn't be on a Saturday night. Warmth of a blood-to-the-groin kind of life is rife in a country town, especially in winter, which is what got Ginger Dawn in the end, so to speak. During the two years and some I was away, I would like to say that my girl had mixed herself up with Bubba Two-Blue out at the roadside tavern or someone named Slim Hambone, a seasonal worker on somebody's farm, it would be a more colorful yarn. But the fact is she took up with Sam Cameron, down at the feed store. A man in his fifties whose wife had died years before, a community pillar, he did the right thing by my girl and married her at the justice of the peace. Now she is big with child, my own string-bean child, her belly out to here carrying my grandbaby, who I will be very curious to see. Ginger Dawn's lively and domestically pleased with herself, her coppery hair a frizz on top, too young to be a Mrs. but proud anyhow of being one. She is eighteen. I can't criticize, never having experienced matrimony. And so I think that my line, as skimpy as I know it to be, is improving due to her attitude, which some might call righteous.

I buried my da in the cemetery near Redwoods Hospital. The location was not a beautiful one, not set next to the ocean, on bluffs with blooming ice plant crunching underfoot or anything like that. It was on a hillside, back beyond a sub-division, at least peaceful, no trucks streaming by. It turned out he was legally married to Bettey Forbert and she knew all along where he was. She didn't tell me because she thought I might claim her house when he died. She thought maybe a daughter had rights over a five-years' wife, and so she was protecting herself, a quality I am coming to admire in a woman.

On my way south, for what I figured would be a brief unwinding, I paid one last visit to the cemetery and walked across the dew-wet grass to the new mound that was him. I circled it the way a dog does, staking territory, and tried a prayer but no words came to mind. And all the while, inside I was burbling with some unexplained joy. A geyser waiting to break through. What I wanted was to fly. Swoop and soar, flutter off, free. So I began, a short burst of out-of-shape hippity-hops that got me a few yards. I raised my arms for flapping, and was revving up again when I glanced at my wings and saw that my hands were trembling, like my da's used to do. I felt watched, but no eyes were on me. They never were. I was as free as I was going to be, except for the booze, as I was coming to realize, that bound me tighter than any past.

It's like having the jaws of a hyena fastened to you when you are trying to shake what you were hoping was only some temporary bad habit. You will do anything to stop the pain caused by those teeth. So you say to yourself, Just a sip, to sleep on; you say, Oh, just one teeny shot; angry, you say, I can do what I want; you say, I don't need this drink, it's the taste I'm after. All of what you read about drinkers is true; we can talk our way into any bottle. I was slow catching on to my tricks, sold the house and everything in it, first to support my addiction and then to rid myself of it. I rented myself a shack outside El Centro, near the Mexican border; and having stocked up on canned and dehydrated foods and bottled water, I took the tires off the truck and tied on the boxing gloves for the long-put-off main event, bouts-to-the-death with my own brain. I weathered, got brown and creased as any geezer.

But the fact is, you get to a certain age in life and you want to belong to something, to some family or some tradition. You get tired of dragging yourself along and trying to keep faith in that. You get to a certain age and your spirit runs out of steam and you realize that this business of being an individual is pretty much a fake. Middle age irons out our details, thick-waists some, bone-and-sinews the rest, but we all tend to look the same, and weary when our guards are down. It gets harder to tell us apart. Ask any young person. Ask Ginger Dawn, she'd be happy to tell you. So you want family then or a church or maybe the Hospital Auxiliary or a choir to belong to; but mostly it's family you want and the sense of who has gone before and who comes after and where you fit in the scheme of things. It's the time of life you wish you were Orthodox Jewish or a Kennedy, before all their troubles.

Now I am living above the hardware store and filling in until a full-time job opens up.

Dot at the drugstore, my second day back, says, "Just goes to show how Ginger missed her daddy, after all", referring to Sam's age and to Bill. Dot is old enough to know better, to have heard the stories. But you live in a town, or some part of you stays in it long enough, and sections of your life become fiction. Certain facts soften around the edges as your name starts to stand for something in the memory of the place.

Right off, I make myself walk by Bill's old house that was then mine, up and down the road, dallying and trying to look interested in the weeds at the edges of the asphalt, or pausing to look skyward like someone studying clouds, for rain or sun or shapes of things to come; but I have that house locked in the corner of my eye and note what has happened to it. They have torn off the veranda that ran along the side and put a big deck in its place with no shade from the sun. The whole thing looks lopsided, the deck as big, I know, as the house's own shadow in summer when the sun would be just south of it. On the deck is a child's sandbox and a little wooden chair painted blue facing where once the garden was, the chair sitting just so, as though a child might at any moment slam the door they've added that leads to the deck and toddle over to the little chair and sit, hands on its little knees, and watch the sun go down over the hill.

The garden is gone, just flowers around the edges now and upstairs, new curtains, big pink and black dots on them, the window made into a bay, something I might have done if I'd had the idea. And they've got those ugly, artificial shingles on the outside, covering real wood. They're too bright a white, those shingles; the house looks out of place squatting in the summer green. Even fresh snow would look soiled next to the gleaming of those shingles.

Every section of my life means starting over and I guess this one's no different. I had something, something real, a house with my name on the mortgage and on the mailbox, and I let it go. Something in me longs for my house back. I will have to guard myself, that I don't become mean-minded as I watch that family growing older in my house and that I don't become bitter enough to poison them and end up a character on the six o'clock news. In the first mornings back I walk along the road and look and remember us there, Bill and me and Ginger Dawn, and I remember Bill holding her up to the old Gravenstein while she picked the green apples big as the palms of her two hands; and I remember Bill in the shed and that little girl on her stool watching him file and sand, making something old, new; making something broken, fixed; making something, a shelf or a bookcase or a chest because I mentioned wanting it for the house. I remember picking all that squash we used to grow and hacking it into triangles and packing it away in the freezer and one winter Ginger Dawn turning yellow and the doctor saying that was why: too much squash pie, among other things. She was three then and greedy. I remember Bill not being there and Ginger Dawn and me for about a year trying to fill the emptiness with our shouting, and then we stopped and took up listening and tried to teach ourselves Bill's mending ways. By that time the house needed it and she was eight and some and handy with a hammer and I got good at plumbing and then she started specializing in picky things, in refinishing window trims and moldings. I sometimes heard her sanding in the night and for a time I thought maybe she was crazy and I was worried and ashamed. But in daylight she didn't seem any worse than anybody else and in time outgrew it.

It's fine and dandy to dally along a road, mooning and bringing tears to your own eyes with your memories, but the fact is the house isn't mine any longer, and the fact is, I am lying. I don't want the old days back. It was the sound of a small plane that did it. That's how noticing is: once something catches your attention, you wonder where you've been all your life.

Connell Field isn't far when you've got a sturdy old truck that still runs. I lean my forehead on the wire fence and stare at a little plane like somebody who has just discovered such things are in the world.

Two fellows come out of the hangar toward the plane, the bright yellow one I've got my eye on. The older man who I sometimes see in the hardware carries a clipboard and his hair in the breeze is grey and longer than I thought now that it's loose. They walk around the plane touching it, feeling the solidness of it, the wires connecting moving parts I don't know what they are called. Then they start sniffing things on that plane.

The nose doesn't lie, you twist the gas spigot, let the gas splat on the asphalt and I am beside them, kneeling down and sniffing, inspecting its iridescent peacock colors on the baked ground. We open the wing-like hood and take the oil stick and run our fingers along it to feel the texture of the grease. We pat the plane warm in the sun, touch its dusty and rivetted metal surfaces, and smell its fluids, as though it is our baby, our first and only born.

11

Lost and Found

Coast Highway

At the bottom of the stairs Dian Lewis, coat thrown on over her night-gown, her feet in thongs, sets off toward the surf, clammy globs of sand mushing between her toes. Pretending she wants to be out this slushy Sunday morning followed by a galloping fifteen-year-old, instead of warm in bed with Duncan, gives her the start of a doozer of a head-ache. The October air is chilly and so wet it's a misty rain. Already her hair feels like tangles of seaweed dangling from her scalp. She pauses to stuff her face with a piece of cold waffle grabbed from the refrigerator. This morning sickness business is for the birds.

Her daughter Andy stops dancing clumsy circles around her, reaches out and touches her cheek. Dian's brittle early-morning nattering at herself cracks; she wants to lie in this big girl's arms and cry. She hasn't told Andy about the baby. That's the purpose of the walk, away from house and Duncan, away from Duncan's waking up and finding out she didn't tell Andy as she promised to, last week while he was away. She didn't tell Andy about the baby because all along she has wondered about miscarrying, hoping that if something, anything, is not one hundred percent about this fetus, then God or the devil will take it, take it soon. She is too old, too tired. She could not deal with another retarded child.

"Something's wrong, Mommy," Andy says.

"Listen, babe," Dian starts. There is something about the clear blue eyes studying her so seriously that stops her tongue from lying, from making up happy fantasies, from carrying out the cheerleader approach she and Duncan decided on. She says, "I want to tell you a secret." She waits, then, to give Andy lead time, watches for the slight frown that indicates a shift in gears. The pretty features that used to remind her of an old-fashioned porcelain doll are becoming coarser, as though slowness of mind eventually affects circulation. Her eyebrows, too, are changing, growing heavy and dark, like her father's.

"What's the secret, Mommy?"

Dian hardly gets a dozen words out when Andy interrupts. "You were keeping secrets from me, Mommy. I knew you were. I'm not stupid, you know, but Duncan, he thinks I am. Stupid. He looks at me stupid. It shows. Like I knew you were lying."

"I wasn't. I just didn't know how you – "

"Duncan yells at me all the time. He yells at me to put away my clothes. He yells about turning down the stereo."

The hidden baby flutters, gut-deep; maybe, she thinks, maybe it wants out. "Listen, babe, I criticize you too when you forget."

"It's different with you, Mommy. You know me. You and me know each other a long time. I mean," Andy steps back, eyes brightening as she recalls what Dian once told her, "you and me have a PAST!"

"Come here," Dian says, opening her arms. "Please."

Andy shakes her head. "I know things, Mommy. About babies. I would like to be alone now."

She turns and begins to run. She runs in the heavy sand with her feet flung out to the side, but in the wintery light misting over the cliffs she looks like Tarzan's Jane in bluejean cut-offs, blond hair flying, legs strong and tanned. Dian watches her until she disappears behind an outcropping of rock.

A wave creeps in, bubbles over Dian's feet, wets the hem of her nightgown. Vague with grief, she starts to cry. Just when she needs the image of Duncan's face, she loses it.

Tylenols. She dips her hand into the tap and gulps the capsules back and lets the water dribble down her chin and throat. In the mirror next to the sink her face is wan, ugly, a green-gilled aging female face. Through the window, however, is a view she never dreamed could be hers, ocean and sky, Monterey Cypress bent in the wind. She has a man. She has money. She has good fortune. She also has nausea and a girl down on the beach who is worried sick. Because that's the way Andy is, she has always worried. "Kids? Kids? You wanna play, kids?" "Mommy, how come the kids won't play with me?" "Mommy, how come teacher don't give me a book and all them, the other kids, got 'em?" "Mommy? My panties got wet at school." "Mommy? What's a dumbo?"

"Mrs. Bell? Andrea is wetting again. And crying in class. You'll have to take her home."

"Mrs. Bell? We'd like to test Andrea to, well, confirm what we suspect."

"Mrs. Bell? We have special classes, you know, for children, well, like Andrea. She would happier there. Less frustrated. A bus would pick her up and drop her back home."

"Mrs. Bell?"

Piss off, Mrs. Bell said, no longer Mrs. Bell. She pulled Andy out of school, left Los Angeles, took a bus north. Settled in a coastal village in the only thing she could afford, a cottage with no electricity, no running water. Put Andy in the local three-room school and found odd jobs waitressing, clerking, pumping gas. Joined the hippie women's quilting bee, the Women's Center. Made a life, so that Andy was accepted, so that Andy was safe.

"Darling? You look lost." From behind, Duncan wraps his arms around her waist, moves his hand down to her belly. "Sick?"

"Your arms are too long," she says, shrugging free.

He moves aside, pours a cup of coffee. "Welcome home, my love.

How was your week in San Francisco? Missed you, sweetheart. I hope the court case went well and the bad guys were sorry. It was wonderful of you to drive home last night through fog, like a madman, because you missed me. You're thinking all those things, right?"

"Right." She punches his chest. "I did miss you. Maybe."

"He'll take whatever kind words he can get. You going to cry now, so happy to see me?"

"No." But she blows her nose and wipes her eyes, then sits at the table and confesses her conversation with Andy on the beach.

Duncan stares out at the grey sky. "I see."

"I should have told her last week," she says. But last week was so peaceful, like the old days, just Andy and her. Without Duncan and Andy at each other's throats.

"Yes, you should have."

Her face burns. His matter-of-fact tone makes her afraid; his initial pleasure at being home is so obviously gone. He's working too hard, he looks like hell. He certainly doesn't need her aggravation. "I'm sorry," she murmurs, distracted, because her headache is suddenly better. She is euphoric, without discomfort for the first time since she got up, but guilty; this baby is fattening on Tylenols and scraps of bread-related carbohydrates. She pushes herself up from the table, swallows a few multi-vitamins. Does it really matter? She fed the unborn Andy on Tiger's Milk hi-protein powder. It's all genes. Genes and fate. She takes milk and eggs out of the refrigerator, starts to make French toast.

Duncan is saying, "I have to be careful with her all the time. I always have to try to anticipate how she'll respond. I might be too old for this."

Dian's stomach plunges to her knees, catapults to her throat. It would be easy for Duncan to leave her. He has a cottage in Tahoe, an apartment in the city. He could just take off. He doesn't need to be hassled by them. In fact, he might regret he ever got involved with them. His life had been orderly. Work and play. One ex-wife from years before, no children. Dian looks at him and feels her eyes bugging out, and it feels awful to her; it feels like begging.

In the afternoon, while Duncan is out strolling on the beach, Andy starts talking non-stop. She is in the dining room talking through the French doors that open onto the deck, talking to Dian who until then was sitting peacefully at the picnic table, bundled in a sweater and drinking ginger ale, face tilted toward the fuzzy sunlight. When Dian tries to dart into the house, Andy clicks the door shut, locking it, and raising her voice, keeps on talking. "I know things, Mommy. You like it in bed with Duncan? You like him to put his thing in you? I know what it's called, you know. Not a penis or whatever like you said. It's called a PRICK! And ladies can only get babies one way – you get away from me, Mommy – but it's okay with me, really Mommy, because I love babies, I really do. And you and Duncan are in love, right? Better than you loved my dad, but that's good, isn't it, it's good for a baby to have lots of love, isn't it, right? Right? Don't you touch me, Mommy. You stay away from me."

Trapped on the deck, Dian recalls a Doberman pinscher she read about who ate a newborn baby because it was jealous. It was a friendly pet, everyone said. Then it turned. Dian tries the door again. Still talking, Andy moves to the living room, takes the photo albums from the hutch. Dian thinks, The kid has turned.

When Duncan comes into view below, she shouts and waves. Then Andy unlocks the door. "I'm so sorry Mommy, I was bad, Mommy." Dian springs inside and bats at her face, sputtering, "Don't you ever! Never again!" and finishes with "And stop calling me Mommy!" She slams a door for emphasis.

By the time Duncan arrives upstairs, the women in his house are wailing. He calls Andy "young lady" and sits her down at the dining room table.

Andy weeps, her fair skin turning blotchy.

Dian tells him not to be hard on her.

"Shit," Duncan says.

Dian is reminded of how Andy's father reacted when he first saw his baby. He had been up north working on the pipeline, making money for graduate school. As far as Dian was concerned, he had taken his time getting back; Andrea was ten days old. "Shit," he said when he saw the baby, because you could tell something was wrong with her, even then. The eyes slanted a bit, as though she had intended to be Mongoloid and changed her mind. Dian (whose name was originally spelled Diane) never forgave him. That Diane began to hate him. It became obvious to her the marriage wasn't going to last.

"Don't you swear in front of my child," she says to Duncan.

On Monday morning, heartburn is already killing her; she lies curled on the bed, arms around her belly. For a change Andy went cheerfully off to school, sensing, Dian supposes, the rift between her and Duncan. Duncan started the day with a speech delivered to her in the bedroom, after which he left, maybe to play squash with a buddy. He didn't say. In the speech he said plenty and what he said was right. Her moods were volatile and she treated him according to how she felt at any given moment. She reprimanded him, right in front of that kid, as he calls Andy. In reply all Dian said was, "She's not 'that kid'," which surprised them both, especially her. She must be entering a masochistic phase, wanting to find out first hand what it would be like, to be pregnant, on welfare, with a mixed-up teenage kid on her hands. "Oh, God," she said. "I'm sorry, babe." He told her not to swear and reminded her that the endearment "babe" belonged to Andrea. Dian then wondered aloud if it was too late to have an abortion. Duncan left the house, to go wherever he went. She crawled onto the bed to curse heartburn and think.

By the time Andy comes through the door after school, Dian is ready for her, sits her down at the kitchen table, feeds her warm chocolate chip cookies just out of the oven. The child is starting to get acne but Dian doesn't care just then, although lately she has spent a fortune on preventative creams.

"This is a ladies' heart to heart," she begins. "Two ladies talking the truth. My turn. You listen."

She tells her daughter about being in love with a man. About jealousy, of a little girl and the man. Who both want the mommy's attention. She talks about being tired. About the pretty house they have now. And the mommy not having to work all the time or worry about money. About how a sweet little baby will be fun. And how the girl can go to beauty school in a few years if she wants to.

To her monologue, Andy says, "I want to go to beauty school now, Mommy. I'm grown up, you know. I have tits and everything just like grown up ladies. You told me. Remember, you told me? And I like babies, you know I like babies because they're so cute and tiny, but this baby is yours, and Duncan is its daddy, it don't belong to me, Mommy. I'm just sort of extra."

"Oh, God."

"You shouldn't swear, Mommy."

"Shuttup, babe. Don't tell me what to do. And stop calling me Mommy."

Andy gets up from the table, her head bowed. "Gimme a hug," Dian says and obediently Andy turns, then throws her arms around her mother.

"I love you Mommy."

"Then be nice to Duncan, babe. Do it for me. Please."

"I love you Mommy."

"I know."

"I love you Mommy." She pulls back and frowns. "Did you forget?"

"Ah. I love you, Andy."

"That's better. I was worried."

"I love you, Andy."

"Can I look at pictures?"

"I love you, Andy."

"Mom-my!"

"I do, you know. Love you."

"Do you love me better than that other baby?"

"Oh, God."

"You shouldn't swear, Mommy," Andy says and dashes out of the kitchen giggling.

Dian sits huddled in a blanket at the top of the stairs that lead to the beach and watches Duncan and Andy below, scuffling figure eights in the sand. Baby talk. Duncan's idea. Occasionally he stoops to inspect a shell, but Andy, who for some reason thinks hunting shells is childish, doesn't join in.

Watching them, Dian thinks a person could go crazy living with the tension between those two big babies. The caffeine in the black coffee she's drinking pumps her up, makes her heart trip over itself, which feels pleasantly dangerous, as though the whole works could suddenly come to a halt. Anxiety is keeping her weight down, a good thing. Duncan isn't the kind of man who would go for a Rubens, even a pregnant one.

Trudging back up the stairs, Duncan shrugs. Andy is pouting. "Well, you guys," Dian says idiotically, leaping up like the leader of a pep squad whose team has just been skunked. "Shit," she says.

"Don't swear," they say in unison and Dian could tumble down the stairs with joy.

A few times a year since she was eight, Andy receives a short letter with a Los Angeles postmark and no return address. A friend of Dian's sends it because of Dian's theory that Andy would feel less dumped by her father. Later in the week Andy announces at the dinner table, "Daddy misses me. Mommy? We have lots of money now, don't we, Mommy?"

"Why?"

"We could send Daddy some money and then he could come and visit us, right?"

"Don't be silly."

"Well, why not, Mommy? You told me we had lots of money. You told me to be nice to Duncan because the house is pretty and costs lots of money. Why can't we send money to Daddy?"

As Andy, sent to her room, stomps out, Duncan waggles his eyebrows at Dian. "Love me for myself, huh?"

Clearing the table, he says, "I married a gold digger. Snafued into a trap by blue eyes, curly hair."

"You're asking for it," Dian says.

"A warm and pleasant disposition."

"I had to think of some damn reason for her to be nice to you."

"A tranquil family life."

"Keep it up, buster. Just keep it up."

"Oh, lady, I will, I will. Later. But you shouldn't have given it to her. The letter. I told you it wasn't a good idea."

"I didn't ask your opinion."

"Ah. That was your mistake. I would have told you it wasn't a good idea."

On Wednesday Andy has the photo albums spread out on the living room rug, again, looking through the pages intently, looking for her history, Dian suspects, the before-Duncan time. The pictures of Duncan and Dian or the three of them together take up only a small section at the end of the last book. Andy peels back the plastic sheets, pulls off pictures and rearranges them. Dian watches her, from the rocker where she is cutting out patches for a baby quilt. When Andy goes to the bathroom, she slides out of the chair and thumbs through the album. Andy as a baby is next to a picture of Dian and Duncan cutting their wedding cake; the baby Andy is in Paris with her own father and Dian before she was even born. Dian thinks a shrink could have a field day with this.

"I was cute, huh?" Andy flops on the rug.

"You still are, babe. But beautiful, actually. Young-woman type beautiful."

"Do you ever wish you never had me?"

"Oh, for God's sake." Dian leans toward her, ready to kiss her cheek.

"Don't," Andy says. "You're always trying to hug me. Duncan says I'm big now. You just said it, too. I'm almost grown up. He's right, too."

Dian squats on her heels and loses her balance. She wobbles over backwards. Andy laughs.

"I'm getting old," Dian says. "I used to be able to sit on my heels like the best of hippies."

"It's the baby, Mommy. The baby makes you sick."

"I'm getting old, is all. Baggy. Saggy."

"Men like young girls, huh. They like to stick their thing in young girls."

"What the hell, Andy. Where do you hear garbage like that?" Dian's skin has gone clammy. She looks at her daughter. Eyes blue as the sea in summer sun. Clear. Empty, really. Lovely. Body like a brick shithouse. Ugly eyebrows, but then look at what's-her-name. Something Hemingway. Face it, Mommy. Look at those painted toenails. No business wearing a T-shirt with no bra. Good God. "Has a boy been touching you?"

"Don't be silly, Mommy." Andy points to one of the wedding pictures. "I look pretty in that dress you got me. The pink goes nice with my hair. You look pretty good yourself, Mommy."

Dian could lay an egg. Talk about changing the subject. She looks at Andy, whose face is smooth and bland as homogenized milk. She looks at the picture. The bride looks good. Ten times better than now; she deteriorated as soon as she was married. In the photograph she and Duncan are holding hands, facing the camera. Andy in her frilly high-necked dress is standing slightly to one side, looking away. Dian had tried to pull her in, but she resisted. The picture makes Dian queasy, but then, everything makes her queasy.

She looks at her wedding ring, a gold band inset with diamonds. No time for an engagement because of the baby, they had a small traditional wedding in the local Methodist Church. Andy told her mother she shouldn't wear white; she was too old. Dian said it was her first real wedding. The stricken look on Andy's face made her wish she had bitten her tongue off at the roots.

"I look kinda left out in this picture, huh?" Andy points. "Like you and Duncan belong together, and I'm just sort of there."

"We didn't want it that way, babe. We wanted us all close. You're the one who backed away."

"That's your story. I know things," Andy says, and flips the album shut. "What are you making?" she asks, glancing at the pastel quilt patches that lie on the rug beside the rocking chair.

While Dian is tucking her in Thursday night, Andy fusses, worrying about a science test she has to take on Friday. She hasn't been listening to the study tapes the teacher gives her, and Dian has forgotten to remind her. It's going to be a timed test, she says, where you have to write things down real fast. "Please, Mommy, please Mommy, can I stay home?"

Friday is stormy, waves and wind. Duncan goes to the Santa Rosa office, and Dian is just as glad Andy is home; she hates storms, the idea of the electricity shutting off any second. Early in the day she locates candles and matches and the kerosene lantern, puts them on the dining room table. She makes lentil soup, does a hand wash. Her ring is on the counter. Andy skips in. "Can I play with your ring, Mommy? It's so pretty. I'll be careful."

Goodbye, ring. Andy screaming when she realized it was missing, Dian thinking at first she had cut off her finger. Could it be in the toilet? Down the sink? Under the bed? Andy doesn't know. She sneaked out the basement door to go outside for a while, she likes wind even if her mommy doesn't, and when she looked for it, later, the ring was gone. Her dolly swallowed it? Don't be stupid, Dian said.

God.

After an exhausting search out in the storm going through handfuls of wet sand, and inside sifting through the contents of the vacuum cleaner bag after vacuuming the whole house, Dian is too numb to cry. She sends Andy to her room.

Duncan is furious. "Do you realize how much that ring cost? and you let that kid play with it? Christ, Dian, what am I to think? How much am I expected to take from you?" He slams the front door. He has never slammed a door before when they've argued. He has never stayed away the night.

Around three in the morning when it's apparent Duncan isn't coming home, she takes a sleeping pill. Even so, she sits hollow and awake by the window and watches the moon over the water.

She wanders, feeling light-headed, drunk, down the hall to Andy's room. The kid is asleep. She shouldn't be asleep. She should be at least half as wretched as she has made her mother. What right has she to be asleep? Dian stares at her, lying on her back, mouth open, hair snarled on the pillow, white moonlight in her face. A woman. A child. A moron. A frigging idiot.

She shakes her awake. She wags a finger in her face and says shrilly: "You're trying to fuck up my marriage, but it won't work, babe. I am keeping this together over your dead body if I have to, you got that? You probably swallowed the frigging ring just to drive me crazy, just to make me so sick I lose this baby you're so jealous of. Oh, God you are such a pain in the neck!" Then she grabs Andy and holds her and beats her fists on that solid back and hugs her and starts to cry.

On Saturday, when Dian wakes past noon with a crashing headache, Andy isn't in her room.

The cupboards spill clothes, but her new designer jeans are missing, the baby locket her grandmother gave her and her laciest underwear are missing; the suitcase Duncan gave her for her fifteenth birthday is gone.

Dian moves very, very carefully through Andy's bedroom, touching things, carefully opening and closing drawers, tallying by rote what is there, what isn't. Andy's smell is on her pillow, her cologne in the stale air of the room. Dian carefully unlatches the window to let in fresh air as she has done nearly every morning since they've lived in Duncan's house. In slow motion she glides through every room of the house and looks for a note on the hall table or beside the phone or held by a magnet on the refrigerator or lying on Andy's favorite windowseat with the best view Andy says, even though it looks out on the fence and the road beyond and the hills beyond that, that reflect the sunsets, Andy liked those reflected sunsets and Dian hears herself thinking in the past tense.

Duncan isn't in either office. He isn't in the San Francisco apartment.

Andy isn't over at any of her friends' houses.

Dian thinks she is going blind.

The ocean slushes, roils in the aftermath of the storm. It's foggy, in billows.

On the beach through binoculars she sees a figure running, long hair flying.

On the highway looking north, looking south she sees a figure running, long hair flying.

A patrol car creeping along in the fog stops. "Anything wrong, Mrs. Lewis?"

She looks down at herself. She is barefoot and her feet are scraped and raw. There is vomit on her robe. She is nowhere near the house.

"Would you like a ride home?"

They are talking softly, treating her as though she is crazy. She runs a hand through her hair that feels slimy. "Yes," she says, answering both questions.

Duncan is waiting. "What the hell?" he starts but then he looks at her. "Christ."

"Maybe she's in Rosy's, having a Coke?"

Dian throws clothes into a suitcase. In the living room Duncan paces, ready to drive her to the San Francisco airport. A girl of Andy's description took the bus inland, toward Santa Rosa. That much they know. The Santa Rosa police are checking with drivers if they remember her getting on another bus. All the connections south leave from there. Her going south is all Dian can think of. No doubt Andy pictures herself stepping off the Greyhound in Los Angeles and simply finding her father there, waiting to meet her, the moment her feet touch L.A. turf. Dian doesn't know if he still lives in Los Angeles; he has no phone, listed or unlisted.

The idea of the child wandering around on her own at the bus depot or drifting naively through downtown streets looking at all the pretty lights drives Dian frantic. Her friend in Los Angeles says she will meet all buses incoming from the north. But what if Andy gets off in San Francisco? Or any one of dozens of stops between? What if her money is stolen (the almost-$80 she took from Duncan's desk)?

What if a boy
please God let it be a boy, but not a psycho boy, God, not one of

those wholesome-looking psychotics with a knife or a hammer, if any-body, God, a nice boy, not one looking for a victim –

God, not a man who sees a pushover in that sweet face, not a cruel man who would hurt her, rape her.

Not a killer, God, please.

In the car whipping down the coast Dian can't talk to Duncan or look him in the eye. She hates her belly, the faint stirrings in her womb. She wants her own yellow-haired girl back.

What if a man tells her child he will show her a good time? (Is that what he would say? Is that what they say today?) Tells her she is pretty? Kisses her cheek, makes her blush?

Leads her off the bus.

Dian has plenty of time to think. On the plane, in police stations. On the streets, looking. In hospitals, looking. In clinics, runaway-counselling offices, on the beaches. During hours on hold, phoning. On the plane back.

In the next room the baby whimpers.

Dian sits on the window seat, stares out at the road. Of course Andy wouldn't write a note. She was always embarrassed by her child-like writing that looked like a chicken did it. A teacher once told her that. Andy didn't forget some things. Andy didn't forget personal things.

It's easy to lose a ring; small, it gets misplaced or rolls into corners, under rugs, buries itself in the sand, disappears down drains, hides in dust balls beneath beds or in the pocket of a doll's apron. Which is where Dian finally found hers. Wadded up in the doll's white lace hanky. She thinks: It shouldn't be so easy to lose a child. But sometimes it's easier. They just go off one day and misplace themselves.

Capricorn Women

Thank you for coming home at this time of need.

That's what Nell's mother, Ellen, tells her when Nell, puffing, falls through the door after three flights of stairs and twenty-two hours on a bus. Her mother involuntarily steps back. Maybe Nell smells. Of the toilet at the back of the bus or the toilet water of the old woman who sat beside her. At least of the greasy french fries and mold-colored pea soup she gobbled in Sudbury.

Nell notices, though, that Ellen has a tiny piece of what might be spinach caught between her pretty incisor and left front tooth. Avidly she inspects her mother for other flaws, but Ellen is still fashionably thin and well dressed, in immaculate, tailored slacks; her hair is a halo of softly groomed golden curls. Nell is disappointed, because she herself is chubby, with round cheeks that make her look younger than she is and eyes that are small and dark and close together, piggy eyes she thinks; her hair, too, is lank and mousy. She takes after her father, a Major General in the U.S. Army; she even has his square military-type body and post-like legs. She jokes that this physical potential for endearing herself to someone in her family was wasted, because her parents divorced and she grew up in Buffalo with Mama-Ellen (her grandmother who is now dying, which is why Nell has come home) and Ellen, both of whom tended toward blond willowiness.

In the foyer with her mother Nell watches herself revert to the well-fed pasty-cheeked child she used to be, the cockroach kind who bided time eavesdropping and dozing in dark closets, and then beetled out into vacated candlelit rooms to snatch petit fours and dainty candies for sucking on privately. She liked the English fruit jellies the best. She disgusted herself. She thrived on her disgust.

Your blouse is wrinkled, Ellen says. Come along dear.

For an instant Nell imagines herself aloof, tall and cool, eyes slightly glazed, removed in philosophical thought. She says, For God's sake Mother I came as soon as I could, taking the bus instead of a plane to save Chuck money because you know how he is and after all this time and the awful trip in those uncomfortable seats and Cynthy turning sixteen and into a bloody monster that's all you have to say to me, my blouse is wrinkled?! Of course it's wrinkled. I've been on a bus for twenty-four lousy hours. God, I just knew it would be awful.

Her mother flinches, lifts a slender shoulder.

Nell sighs. I'm sorry, Mother. It's been hard for you.

Ellen's arthritic, manicured fingers flutter near Nell's shoulder. Her silver bracelets jingle in Nell's ear. Nell's knees quiver as she leans toward the hands. Her mother swoops up Nell's suitcase which is held together with wide packing tape.

Uh, let me, Nell says.

But the bag and her mother are halfway down the hall to Nell's old room.

For as long as Nell can remember, Mama-Ellen has lived one floor below, in the second-floor apartment. On the first floor is a retired professor of Oriental languages, who keeps to himself. After showering, Nell tiptoes downstairs to visit Mama-Ellen without her mother butting in. Passing through Mama-Ellen's dining room she spies the mahogany table, chairs, and china cabinet. Unlike the rest of the furniture, oak and massive, the mahogany pieces are delicate. Nell's eyes gleam. The mahogany set is classy, would fit beautifully in her dining room in their new house outside Thunder Bay.

In the bedroom she stands wide-eyed, marvelling over Mama-Ellen. Nell thought dying people shrank, but Mama-Ellen's as big as a beached whale. For the first time Nell recognizes a resemblance between herself and the women in her family.

Mama-Ellen, she says in a whisper.

For landssake don't whisper. I'm not dead yet. About time you showed up. You come home finally to see your grandmommy die. Good, good.

Nell doesn't say Thank you. She stops herself in time. Are you in pain?

And shouldn't I be?

Nell grabs the hand that has grown bloated, familiar rings cutting into swollen flesh.

She hears her mother enter the room. She smiles, squeezes her grandmommy's hand.

The hand squeezes back.

Nell's eyes smart. She sniffs.

Is that girl crying? Mama-Ellen asks her daughter.

Yes, Mama-Ellen, she is. Ellen raises her eyebrows.

Nell swallows snot.

I suppose when she goes I'll know it. I'll feel something strange, Ellen says over tea at the mahogany table.

Nell runs her hands on the dustless, shiny table top. Her daughter Cynthy's traitorous letter, detailing Nell's faults for the last fourteen years, is burning a hole in her brain. To distract herself, she wonders how she is going to keep the table so polished. She's not good with furniture.

Ellen cocks her head. You want it, don't you?

Nell looks out the narrow cut-glass window above the china cabinet. Uh, no, not really.

Good. Because you're not getting anything, my dear. You have to wait until I go. It'll be fun.

Nell imagines herself laughing, a tinkly lady-like sound, her eyebrows arching at the humor of her own witty remark. She says, What are you talking about, what do you mean? What're you going to do with all this stuff and your place is already packed with great things? You never gave me anything decent, some silverware once that wasn't even silver, you sent somebody to K-Mart for it or something for criminey sakes, all I want is this frigging table that you have no use for. I deserve something. You never give me anything.

No need to be excessive, Nell. Mama-Ellen will hear you.

Nell glances guiltily over her shoulder. Oh, heck, she says.

In the plush eiderdown of the bed Nell sees herself sunk like a plump raisin in the belly of the Pillsbury Doughboy. She blames this bed on her failure in life. With such comfort, why get up? On the other hand, her mother has a normal twin bed, with firm mattress and a no-nonsense ribbed cotton bedspread. A puritan bed that doesn't undermine the sleeper's ambition by being too cozy. Her mother did this to her after Billy died. Compensation? Reward? Nell doesn't know.

No simple drowning, not for their family. No ordinary car accident involving a wholesome boy in a baseball cap struck down on the corner of Main and Burb. No normal childhood leukemia. Billy was a kid manic-depressive. He did what ordinary kids do when wearing a Superman cape. Except he didn't even have the cape. He just figured he could fly if he wound himself up enough by racing through the apartment, and then he sailed out his open bedroom window.

He was smart. A genius-type kid. Nell knew she wasn't very smart. Kind of ordinary. Still alive.

You didn't, uh, encourage him, did you?

She was older and therefore responsible. It was her bad luck she and Billy were home alone. Mother and Daddy were downtown fighting it out at the lawyer's.

Who asked her the question? Daddy? Mother? Oh, probably a cop. They hung around for days. Probing her. You, uh, didn't give him the idea he could fly? You, uh, didn't push him, thinking he could fly because he told you he could?

I'm just dumb, not crazy, Nell said once.

That sounds like a pretty smart answer to me, the cop said.

Thank you, Nell smiled, showing him her missing front tooth. She was eight and slow in losing her front teeth. Billy was six. He had a full set of permanent chompers. Except, Nell thinks now, he didn't last.

God could get her for that. She snuggles down in the fresh sheets. If she thinks about it, she recognizes she's a tragic figure. Always guilty. Guilty for just being alive. Tears squeeze out the corners of her eyes, roll down her temples, mingle with the strands of hair wadded against the pillow.

She can't remember much of the day her brother died. She only remembers afterwards when they plied her with chocolates and bought her things. That lasted awhile, probably until they realized she wasn't going to change. Confess or get smarter, either one. The fact is, they liked him better. He was skinny. Smart. Big-eyed. Nice to old people. She often wished him dead.

In the kitchen leaning over the sink with her face in a third of a honeydew melon Nell ponders. She has been a social worker. She knows something about sibling accident/murders. In one of her cases, the boy left at home dropped the newborn and crushed its skull and was guilty about it years later. She herself doesn't feel guilty, really, except when she's being a bit dramatic; therefore, she must be innocent of the deed. She is gobbling to beat the cook who shows up at 4:30. It is now 4:25. While her mouth is filled with slurpy green juice she forgets about Cynthy's nasty letter burning a hole in her purse.

Knowing the exact time could be significant when someone is on a deathbed; Nell, who likes mysteries, is cognizant of that. But it's not the case with her, she is simply aware of time; she is always trying to sneak in a little extra in her life.

He was too little to open the window himself, Mama-Ellen says. Did you do it?

Her eyes are shut. The strawberry-colored drapes are closed against the night air. The black night nurse has moved discreetly out of the room. Nell feels set up. For years nobody has mentioned how Billy died.

Compulsively she inches toward the bed. The old woman smells like the stems on picked flowers that have been left too long in a vase, a fetid, slimy smell. Nell takes one step back, stretches out her hand, touches her grandmommy's lying swollen and dark as a sausage on a white quilt.

Don't cozy up to me, Nell Ellen.

Nell's eyes fix on herself in a brass-framed mirror above the bed. She looks guilty as hell. Pale. Sweat beading her brow. Her heart starts to pound. She thinks, How dare you ask me such a question, after all these years, who do you think you are, you disgusting, bloated grandmommy! Taking advantage of being sick to be rude! You have no idea what Cynthy has become, your own sweet little great-grandbaby like you used to call her, you have no idea what I've been through!

Um, I don't think so, she says aloud, wondering if she did open the window.

It probably doesn't matter.

That said, Mama-Ellen starts to shake. Nell watches her quiver like a jellyfish stranded on a beach. Her eyes roll. Turn away, she commands Nell.

Nell obeys.

Mama-Ellen moans.

Nell's heart thumps. Nurse! yells Nell. Nurse! Nurse!

You disappoint me, says Mama-Ellen, clear as day. Always have.

Nell turns back, stares at her grandmother whose eyes are closed. Mama-Ellen is covered with sweat; water stands in the folds of her neck.

The nurse bathes her face with a damp washcloth. It's awright, honey, the nurse says. She just get these l'il 'tacks and then she be fine. You gowan now.

Nell doesn't want to go anywhere. She wants to know what Mama-Ellen meant by "It probably doesn't matter." She is wobbling on one foot, considering what to do.

Will you gowan now chile? the nurse says. Don't you worry none about your granny. Shoo now.

Reluctantly Nell slumps out of the sick room, shuts the door. She isn't worried about her "granny" at all. She is worried about herself. She wants to know how Mama-Ellen can talk with her mouth shut. She wants to know if she's hearing things. And she's miffed at being bossed around like a child by a hired nurse. An imposter who's laughing up her sleeve, talking all this old black talk when she's white as cream with a splat of coffee in it and looks, to boot, no older than Nell herself.

She slams the front door and walks at a fast clip around the block. When she returns, her mother answers the bell. How nice you're getting exercise, Ellen says. The pounds will just start to melt away.

Nell's lips tighten. Mother?

Yes dear? Ellen has started back to the livingroom, heels clacking on entry hall tiles.

Mother, I –

Ellen stops, blinks once, twice, eyebrows high.

Nothing, Nell says. She is going to her room and sink her teeth into the tiny jelly beans she found in a gallon jar pushed to the back of the top pantry shelf. They are crusty on the outside and eight colors, although she hasn't taken the time to separate them all into like piles. She clunks down the hall to her room, her work cut out.

Ellen has told the nurse to notify them if Mama-Ellen starts slipping. Around three in the morning Nell is awakened by a rhythmic thud-thud under the floor, a broomstick, as it turns out, held by the nurse standing on a chair.

Nell is drugged by two 30 mg Dalmane sleeping capsules. When the thudding continues, she rolls out of bed to her knees and listens, ear pressed to floor. Her consciousness somewhere between waking and sleeping, she thinks it's Mama-Ellen's spirit knocking to get out. This idea gets her adrenalin, if not her brain, going.

The lamp is on in her mother's room but there's no answer to Nell's tap. Timidly but reminiscently excited, reminded of the time she caught her father bare-bummed, bending to pick up his shorts from the floor, she turns the doorknob, trying to remember how old she must have been, bum-at-eye-level tall. The door opening, Nell descends into herself at five, ten, fifteen: Mommy, Mommy let me in. Gimme, Mommy, gimme. She pictures herself rippling like a mongoose might into her mother's private sanctum, beady eyes gobbling secrets. But there are only playing cards spread out on the bed in messy solitaire rows. What does Nell expect? A lover stashed under the covers? It would have been nice to catch Ellen snoring, saliva dripping out of a corner of her mouth. She would have liked that.

The bathroom door is ajar. She hears her mother fart. Snoring is one thing, farting another. Nell is so embarrassed she backs out and races on tiptoe to her room, where the thud-thud starts up again.

Nell feels creepy. She finally does what she thinks Ellen expects of her. She starts yelling.

Mama-Ellen, meanwhile, has died peacefully, "jest heah one minute, gone the next," the nurse reports. Exasperated, Ellen wants to know why she didn't just come upstairs and ring the bell.

The dead shou'n be left by theyselves. Theys lonely enough as it is.

The answer sounds fair enough to Nell, who gives it some thought.

Her brother had a shock of medium, nothing-much brown hair that grew straight from his crown and out over his forehead like a diving board. Mother was always putting Brylcream in his hair to make it curve over his forehead, and Billy always had a greasy forehead when she finished with him. He waggled his eyebrows like W.C. Fields. He was pigeon-toed. He had nightmares. Had her brother, flattened, been lonely down on the sidewalk?

In Mama-Ellen's living room, after viewing the body one last time, Ellen and Nell drink tea by candlelight. In the forefront of Nell's mind is the image of Mama-Ellen's spirit departing. The spirit would have been a brownish color because she thinks Mama-Ellen most likely had a heavy-duty spirit. She pictures a turd-colored puff exploding out of Mama-Ellen's forehead and heaving itself upwards.

Well, Ellen says. You'll take care of the arrangements. I will not go in there until it's time to sort. A simple burial, Nell. No funeral.

The tips of her fingers, hard as drawer-pulls, brush Nell's bare arm.
Ellen says, I'm sure you can manage. It runs in the family.

Nell sits up straighter. Ellen sighs. I never thought she would actually go. She took enough time. She's been dying for years.

I guess we all do, Nell says.

You have no idea what it's been like. Ellen's hand holding the tea cup starts to tremble. Tea spills in the saucer. She reaches toward the carved coffee table, misses the edge. The half-filled cup of tea overturns onto the carpet, splattering the intricate tendrils of the Persian with ugly brown.

Ellen giggles. It's a good thing Mama-Ellen didn't live to see this. She would have like to kill me.

She sails out of the room. Nell assumes she is getting a rag to wipe up and waits, listening to her mother's surprising giggle floating around the dark room. For a moment her voice even had its old Kentucky twang. The mantel clock strikes the half hour, resumes its secretive, ruminative ticking. Nell realizes her mother isn't coming back.

Nell now listens when she wakens in the night. She hears the shuffling of cards, like muffled shots raddadadading down the hall.

On sorting day, on the landing outside of Mama-Ellen's door are cardboard boxes marked "Rummage" and "Mine" that Nell has scavenged, dragged up the stairs and stacked. (Kitchen odds and ends she is sure Ellen will give her. Nell, not proud, will take what she can get.)

Ellen unlocks the door, stands on the threshold. You know how many times I've done this? Opened this very door and called out Mama? Mama?

Nell's boxes bang against her thighs as she struggles through the door. She stands in the polished dark-wood foyer waiting politely for Ellen to answer herself. Ellen disappears around a corner, into the kitchen.

Well, how many? Nell asks, following. How many times do you think?

How many times what? Ellen's chin is propped on her fingers, her arm against her chest. She is staring at the top cupboards, her mouth pressed in at the corners. She says, I suppose now I'll have to have a tenant in here or sell everything, why not? Or just let it sit, a mausoleum to Mama-Ellen. You know. While I ramble around upstairs going quietly daft?

Nell looks at her mother's fingers that are so thin her rings slip up and down between the joints when she moves. Her hands look gnarled, old. Nell wants to cry.

Ellen glances at her daughter, snorts. Grow up, Nell, she says.

Cynthy wrote me a letter. In it she says awful things. About me. Nell's bottom lip quivers as she speaks.

Oh, *those*. Capricorn women are wonderfully good at writing earth-shaking letters. You realize of course that we all are? Capricorn? I've always found that interesting.

The letter was shocking.

Of course it was. She's sixteen. What else have they got to do at sixteen?

Plenty, Nell snarls.

Oh, *that*. As long as she doesn't get pregnant. That would be dumb. She'll get tired of it, don't you think? Didn't you?

Nell blushes under the roots of her hair. Uh, I, she says miserably, squeezed between a rock and a hard place. Surely Ellen remembers that Nell was "dumb", got caught. She was dumb but isn't tired of "it". Her mouth won't open. Instead, her hand shoots out for the silverware drawer, just as Ellen reaches for it. Their hands touch. Oh, excuse me. Sorry. Nell retreats.

Ellen lifts out the drawer, lets the contents clatter into a box marked Rummage.

Well? Didn't you?

Wait, says Nell. I want that egg beater.

Ellen's eyebrows slowly arch. Of course. The egg beater, she says, and picks up the eggbeater between two fingers, drops it into Nell's box.

It's, uh, antique, mutters Nell.

Vermouth and lemon over ice at midday break turns Nell into an alcoholic of the future; she realizes she won't have to worry about time on her hands in her old age. Cocky with insight, she asks her mother, What will you do?

Do? Ellen echoes. What I have always done. Manage, of course.

Nell, feeling bold and suddenly grown up, pours herself another drink. That's not what I mean, Mother.

Ellen regards the rim of her glass. You always were such an unhappy girl.

Nell staggers to her feet, raises her chin imperiously. Mother. My childhood has nothing to do with it. I'm asking you an adult question. Have you any plans.

Sit down, Nellie, really. What I do, if you mean will I travel or mope or shop twice a day instead of once, is of little consequence. I took care of Mama-Ellen for sixteen long, long years and with my freedom, as you will undoubtedly call it, I will most likely choose to live out my life. Now sit down and behave in a civilized manner.

Nell does.

Mama-Ellen was always happy you turned out all right.

I did? Nell thinks of herself as unfinished. That others see her as a *fait accompli* is startling.

She wanted to have seen more of Cynthy, though. She always talked about Cynthy. Her only great-grandchild.

Yeah, well, Nell says, thinking how Cynthy hated Mama-Ellen. Lips like a sucker fish, the brat said, impertinent nine. She deserved more thrashings than she ever got. And Chuck never would lay out a penny to send her for a visit. Mama-Ellen's the one with all the dough, Chuck liked to say. She wants to see the kid, let her finance it. Cynthy was not Chuck's. Chuck never figured it out. Consequently, Nell never pushes him.

Yeah, well, she says again.

I'm so glad we sent you to college, Ellen says. It made you so articulate.

Cynthy's on the pill. She's screwing some punk weirdo until all hours. Sometimes she stays out all night.

Didn't we all?

Nell pushes her chair back, knocks over her glass of Vermouth. The lace tablecloth soaks up the red. I hate you Mother! Do you hear me? I hate you!

Of course you do, dear. We all hate our mothers. Ellen stands, pats the corners of her mouth and sails out of the room. Nell is left hyperventilating by the fireplace.

The next day they start on the linen cupboards.

Nell, having finished all the purloined jelly beans during the night, feels bloated. She thinks her neck has added a roll. Her eyes have disappeared in the pale puffy moon of her face.

From the footstool she's using to reach the top shelves, Ellen says, Big night last night?

Nell blinks. Yeah, she says.

And snorts.

That's a disgusting sound.

Snort, snort, snort, goes Nell. She starts dancing to the snorts, contorting her square-rigged body. In the middle of a piece she has already decided to call The Pig Dances she says, I think I'm sick.

Her brain is hot. Her head is dizzy. Her stomach roils. Did you love him? she is asking Ellen. Did you? Did you? She may be on the rug, writhing. She may be passed out and floating up to heaven. It's soft wherever she is. Did you love Billy, Mommy?

Who is this ugly thing climbing out of her mouth? Of course Mommy loved Billy. She calls him Billy Boy. Daddy calls him Billy Boy-o. His nurse calls him Good Boy Billy. Billy's a good boy. Like hell, Daddy shouts. Did you love Billy, Mommy? Some bad girl is asking a nasty question. Be quiet Grandmommy says. Shame on you. Oh sure. She's full of shame, fat with it.

Nell is sick. Cool hands put damp cloths on her forehead. Mommy? Mommy?

I'm here.

Did you love Billy?

What a question.

Did you?

He was sick.

Did you love Billy?

He was crazy.

Nell is sick. Billy jumps on her bed, makes her cry. Billy locks the bathroom door and won't come out. Nellie wets her pants outside the door. She is too ashamed to move. Daddy lifts her away later. The carpenter does something to the door. Billy has his head in the toilet bowl. He's not dead.

Nell is sick. Billy is in his own bed across the hall. He has his eyes open but he won't talk. Hi, Billy, wanna play poker? Hi, Billy, wanna eat cake? Hi, Billy, wanna wanna? But Billy isn't home. He is gone for a long time.

Nell is better. She's older. She opens her eyes. God. She's in Mama-Ellen's bed, a deathbed, wearing one of Mama-Ellen's old nightgowns. She smells like dried up lilacs, dusty roses. The pillow smells like dead hair. Mother! Mother! Aaaaaa! Nell flaps around, but she's too weak to do much but muss up the quilt.

Calm down, Nell. For heaven's sake.

But but but, Nell sputters.

Nellie. I couldn't get you any further. You're not exactly skin and bones.

Did you love Billy?

Don't be stupid.

Did you love him?

Of course. He was my son.

Did you love him?

Ellen abruptly turns to leave the room. You always did have a vicious streak, she says.

The door slams.

Ah. Instantly Nell feels better.

Then she's attacked by the dry heaves. Leaning over Mama-Ellen's toilet bowl she suspects she deserves whatever she gets.

His body is small on the pavement. Not that far down, only three flights, and she can see him perfectly, on his tummy wearing the navy blue school jacket he liked so much. Nyahnyahnyah, she said, leaning out. You can't fly, smarty pants.

Nell is crawling back to bed trying not to rip the nightgown under her knees when Ellen, bracelets jingling, returns, dressed in the cream suit Nell's seen her wear to church. Looking down at Nell she says, You're just bothered by what you consider to be an appalling letter from your daughter. You feel you've failed because you've used mother-hood as an excuse to do nothing else with your life. Your ego is upended and protesting. You see, I've done some reading too. And have you forgotten your letter to me? You moved in with your pair of pants, my dear. Put your name next to his on the mailbox for all to see! You want to read that letter? I found it yesterday.

Nell, on all fours, has been stopped in her tracks. Her mother is rigid with anger, something Nell has seldom seen. She doesn't think she wants to read her letter. She was, after all, in college, in the brief playing-at-intellectual period of her life. The letter took days to write. She crafted it precisely, to do the most damage quickly.

She crawls over to her mother. Get out of my way, she says, or I'll piss on your leg.

A choking sound emits from her mother's throat. You are so utterly ridiculous.

Yeah, Ma, says Nell.

In another case she heard about, a boy of six shot and killed his brother, eight. Deliberate or not? The boy wouldn't, or couldn't, tell. Nell hangs over the ledge of the window her brother sailed out of. He was small-boned, blue-eyed. She held him in her arms once while he cried. She wasn't all bad. She thinks she did open the window.

Waiting at the bus depot with the doors of the BMW locked after Nell has bought her ticket, Ellen says suddenly, I want to be cremated. No funeral. Absolutely not. You hear me? And if I ever get sick, no hospitals. And if I can't be dealt with at home, no life-support systems in the extended care. You have my permission to pull any plugs you can get your hands on. You can smother me with a pillow in my sleep if you like. You understand?

Nell understands very well. She looks forward to it.

And buy yourself a decent suitcase. That one is disgusting.

Through the greasy window of the bus Nell watches Ellen, a statue around which passengers dragging bags and squalling kids ebb and flow, looking out of place and greenish under the fluorescent platform lights. She is staying until it's time to give the tight-wristed little wave Nell receives every time she leaves home. Ellen has hollows under her eyes. Nell hears the cards whirring in the night, the sound of her mother waiting for dawn, for death, for time to go by.

Preacher's Geese

Today, though, if she were taking the child home for lunch she would feed her real food, homemade chicken soup with 18% cream stirred into it and juicy bits of white meat and on the side a crusty Parker House roll warmed up from last night's batch, oozing with butter; real food, not those margarine sandwiches and soft little skimpy bruised apples and chemical cellophane-wrapped cakes her mother gives her. If she were taking the child home today, she would pull her out of the classroom on some excuse – she could get away with it, she's a special reading teacher – and buckle her safely, oh we would want that sweet child to be safe, safe, into the car and drive carefully all the way back to civilization, quasi-civilization anyway, and then the child would see, with her own eyes, why she should learn to read, what her future could be if she could read and learn: a nice house could be hers, a dishwasher, real silver on the table, sets of fine china for every occasion. People don't have to live six to a single-wide trailer, people don't have to, for one thing, make babies all the time like her mother, she would see that there are other things in life. And other things besides pigs, which is kind of cute, the way the child, so delicate herself, wispy blond hair, pale sprinkling of freckles like cinnamon across the bridge of her nose, loves her pigs and wants, with an endearing naivety, to be a pig farmer when she grows up. Although Preacher says she can't, because girls can't be pig farmers, which is enough, Lenore thinks, spinning the black Toyota into the school grounds, to make her side with the child. Oh, yes, girls can.

This morning, though, Elsbeth Jane stomps into the room, dragging her dirty Cabbage Patch look-alike doll by one foot, and slams the door. Inside Lenore's dress, underneath the featherweight, so-called, girdle, her belly moves, and the movement is like a flutter of new life in her womb. She thinks it's the morning's laxatives going to work, but then it knots and descends and Lenore realizes her period, erratic beast these days, is starting.

Oh, it's not Lenore's first parent visit that has the child so upset, it's her pigs. One of her six weaner pigs is being sent away to live on a farm in Vancouver or so they tell her. He has a hernia, they tell her, and has to have an operation and that's why Preacher this very day is taking him away in a truck. She has kissed him goodbye on his pukey wet snout, he was the smallest, the runt, she says, and she's worried because she has heard of Vancouver, it's the city of sin Preacher says, so why would they take her dear little pig there?

Vancouver to Lenore is heaven compared to this stinky coastal backwater Jack insisted they move to. "He'll be happy there, I was," she says, and then, heaven forbid, tears are rolling down her cheeks, what a mess she is today.

Lenore doesn't know all the rules in this school district, but she vaguely thinks it's against the law to take a child in your car without parental consent, for one thing, or without it being a designated school trip, but who knows? Everything is different here, maybe nobody up here cares what you do or how you live, they are all so damned depressed, their poverty, their unemployment, their general backwardness, even their damned sky which is grey all the time and dribbling, rain like pee, no city lights to break up the monotony, no plays to make one laugh, no reason to dress up even, no reason period. Jack likes it; as the town's only dentist he can be a big man, already president of the Chamber of Commerce, a force to contend with, he calls himself, chuffing a bit of a self-conscious laugh, but meaning it, she knows him. "You'll get used to it, Old Buddy," he says, leaving the crusts of his raisin bread on the plate, busily stuffing his briefcase with reminders and brochures, patting her shoulder on his way out. Old Buddy, indeed.

The excitement of having the child in the car makes Lenore's brain blank the short distance between the school and the white single-wide trailer mounted atop concrete blocks where Elsbeth Jane lives, the trailer set at an odd, random-seeming angle, on the edge of a swampy field. The smell of sulphur sea in the air is awful, it's brackish, the land, you couldn't grow anything on it. Approaching, you can spot the junk around the trailer, machinery scavenged from the mill, logs strewn about, the children must use them for play, a rusted, wheelless bicycle propped against the propane tank strapped to one end of the trailer, no tarp, of course, over the little stack of firewood that has been cut. In back of the trailer is a shed, a makeshift thing, warped half-planed logs and mill ends. She pulls into what might be the driveway, there are ruts anyway, and as she gets out of the car, the mother is peeking from around a vinyl-backed drape in what will turn out to be the bedroom, Lenore has seen enough of these units to know. She knows it's the mother, Darleen, because she stopped by once, attempting to establish contact between home and school, and was met by a slit-open door, the girl-faced woman peering through, piles of laundry blocking the passage, baby crying, the odor of dirt and male sweat assailing Lenore's nostrils, a fragrance she does not want to think about.

Today, again, the woman doesn't come out to greet her, although two boys, five-year-old twins, dart out from behind the trailer and turn and dart back, giggling and pointing, Lenore hates them suddenly for the pointing, but Elsbeth Jane in her gumboots takes her by the hand and leads her through the wood shavings and muck to the shed where the "dear littles" are kept. Lenore thinks she may faint from the stench in the dark interior of the shed but for the sake of

Elsbeth Jane she smiles, squeezes her hand, starts oh-ing even before her eyes have adjusted to the lack of light.

At the sight of Elsbeth Jane the pigs crowd around squealing, pushing against their small enclosure, and the other creatures, chickens and geese, penned in the shed are set off, squawking and clucking. Chaff floats in the air. Elsbeth Jane claps her hands. "What pretty noise!" she says, and then shyly to Lenore, "Do you like it?"

"I do," Lenore says, "because you do." She wants to say more, about that's how it is with friends or people you love, something she wants to say, but the child has turned again and is leaning over the pig pen, pulling ears and petting her "prides and joys". But, she explains, she doesn't give them names no matter how dear, because a pig is a pig. "Pigs are for eating, that's why God made 'em. You grow 'em, you kill 'em, and you eat 'em. That's what Preacher says." And then she asks if Lenore would like to pet one and Lenore wouldn't, not really, she is unused to pigs, but she thinks they're very nice, very special, very nice indeed. "You know my brothers? The ones that run when they seen you? They ain't even in school yet and they write their names real good. But I'm pretty, aren't I? Preacher says I'm pretty, he says girls don't have to read or nothing, they just got to birth babies for the Lord and my time is coming." She pivots and raising her face to Lenore, lowers her voice. "You know what? Mum's big with child again, he got her by the sink, I seen it. Most of 'em die, though." She covers her mouth, eyes bright above a dusty hand, then cocks her head, suddenly hostessy. "Would you like a stool? Would you like to sit down?" and dashes to drag a stool from somewhere, but Lenore is still back with "he got her by the sink". Who? The father? Preacher? One man or the other it was, who came at the woman, unzipped and ready in the child's presence, apparently, and lifted her dress, perhaps pulled her back by the hips from where she stood at the sink? to make her bend over, her hands still dangling in the soapy water, holding a bowl, a spoon, a knife? A certain kind of woman she would be, who lets things take their course, her hands in warm water, absently rubbing the cloth over whatever it is she holds. A certain kind of woman so used to love-making, maybe, if that's what this is called, so used to, well, say it, fucking, that she even comes quickly, glazed-eyed as a bitch in heat, and then, while waiting for him to finish, turns on the tap and rinses a dish.

"– sit down?" the child is saying and Lenore smiles, oh, and sits, tentatively, testing the legs, and pulls her skirt into her lap to keep it from the dirt and cedar-chip floor, which is, at least, dry in spots although it's obvious the roof leaks, you have only to look up. There is straw and mud and God knows what else stuck on her sensible shoes, she forgot to brush off the seat, she feels silly perched up on this little stool, oh, it doesn't matter, what matters is, leaning forward, asking, "You said they die?" and wondering what in the world the child really has seen, what in the world. It's dirty here, something dirty's going on. She would give her eyeteeth, her eyeteeth, Lord, to remove this one little girl from the primitive environment she was born into, with its coarse, uneducated people, where things happen in a kitchen that a youngster shouldn't know about, much less see. But she needs to find out, if there's abuse here, if – "You said they die?"

"Oh, the babies. Mum don't 'specially want lots but Dad does, he keeps givin' 'em to her anyway, but mostly they get halfway –" one of the pigs starts up, a raspy full-throated squealing, and Elsbeth Jane slaps it on the snout – "then die and Mum flushes 'em or Dad buries 'em and once, one got borned and Preacher baptized him, we just keep getting boys here, even though he was dead from the cord and now Mum has her hopes up again. She says this one's a keeper. It's special. Pigs like it, too. I watch 'em doing it, they got to be older though. I got three boys and three girls, except for the one gone off to be happy in Vancouver, like you. It's a boy."

Lenore is dizzy, there are spots before her eyes. The odor and the undercurrent of satisfied snorting and grunting from the pigs and a sort of busy rustling behind her from the other creatures in the shed is so bad she wants to leave, stand up and just leave, but Elsbeth Jane is happy, stroking the pigs, chatty and grinning over her shoulder at Lenore, and Lenore has her job to do, she needs to know things. Once the child says "Shoo!" and tosses a chunk of wood that bonks against the back wall, at the boys peeking through a slit, making Lenore clutch at her heart. She was lost in revery, there, for a moment, but she does wonder. She's curious and anybody would be: "How do you, how do you tell whether your pigs are boys or girls? I mean, I suppose you can. Tell."

Giggling, Elsbeth Jane tiptoes over and cups Lenore's ear. "Boys have those things, like twigs, that get hard. All boys got 'em. Mum calls 'em honey-sticks, but don't tell Preacher."

The boys come back, thunking rocks against the shed, and yell, "Mum says bring her on in." Lenore, her hand about to touch the child's sweet face, stands, upsetting the stool.

But of course she must see the geese first, the child insists. The two dozen or so white geese crammed in a pen start scuffling, wings pushing wings, pecking at each other's necks and making honking noises when Elsbeth Jane reaches into a feed sack. It takes Lenore a minute to realize their wings are clipped, which explains why, with no chicken wire over the pen like the scrawny chickens have, they don't just fly away. As Elsbeth Jane throws them some dried corn, she says they're having a killing when the rain stops, but until then the geese have to stay in because Preacher wants the feathers nice. She says that she's hoping for the killing because last year she looked in the garbage can and realized about insides. She says, "You take their necks and wring 'em like Levis and then you ax 'em on a stump, that one out there, whop, and the blood shoots out in gushes going bang, bang, bang, all over the dirt and the men are laughing, Preacher too, and the head lies there on the ground and the eyes close real slow."

Lenore turns to look through the doorway, at the stump the child has pointed to, and imagines the wild flapping of wings and the blood and the men laughing.

Boys are different. Boys are disappointing and angular. They push away when you want to hug them. Soon enough boys smell of dirty jeans and unwashed hair. They stay out to all hours, they come home stinking of beer and sometimes girls. Their underwear in the laundry basket is stiff with it, their uncontrollable juvenile sex. What is it with them? What is in boys that transforms them from sweet little things, she remembers Gary at two, three, four, he was sweet, his firm staunch little legs running, running, the way his cheeks became patchy red when he was excited, it almost looked like a rash, people commented on it, and then one day he picked up a piece of driftwood, they were on a picnic, Jack, smoking, gazing out to sea and she building a sand castle trying to interest the child, he picked up a piece of wood, bent in the middle, a boomerang sort of shape really, and turned it into a gun, bang, bang he said, da-da-dat-dat, you're dead. What makes boys do that? What made Jack smile and shoot back with his fingers, pa-choo, pa-choo, and the two of them laugh, the boy and the man, leaving her with her foolish half-built castle, an outsider?

In her bedroom Lenore wonders what to say to Gary, now on unemployment in Vancouver, thinking about moving here. No, she doesn't want it, this heavy-set crude twenty-year old that is her son, no way, as the kids used to say. Even after three months here she has boxes still to unpack, they line the back wall of the walk-in closet, are stashed in the room they call locally the "rec" room, she can't seem to get moved in. The overhead light in the master bathroom needs a fixture, the trashburner has made smoke marks on the kitchen walls, oh, who cares. Her feet hurt, her back hurts, crammed at that dinky table in the trailer kitchen earlier, menopause has made her sweat, like a pig, just like one of Elsbeth Jane's pigs, menopause and tension, that's it, her body smell is changing, it smells old, an old female smell, it has been a long, hard day. Talking to Darleen was like talking to a brick wall.

She stares into the full-length mirror hanging on the door. In the last year or so Jack has touched her, made love to her, less than a dozen times, and fast, with his eyes closed. When she faces sideways to the mirror, her belly is so big she looks pregnant, and far gone, too. Bigger than Darleen, with her stupid knobby little bump, her sleepy eyes with their slightly Oriental cast, her red henna hair in bulky curls around her thin weaselly face. Not at all like bright-eyed Elsbeth Jane, thwarted in that place, with those people.

You must not try to teach her. That's all Lenore went there to say, but the work of it, explaining what a learning disability in a bright child is to a parent like that, trying to explain how endless copying (most of it backwards anyway) night after night doesn't do any good, does, in fact, do harm. The weight of her and what she needed to say to that young woman making the trailer shake as she came down the narrow hall, impossible not to whump, whump even when barefoot, out of respect she had removed her dirty shoes, whumped awkwardly down the hallway, nyloned thighs going swish swish, the bunions so obvious, so exposed, the little rip where one pinkie poked through embarrassing.

Darleen, wearing a bright-orange ruffled homemade blouse, had made instant coffee and set the mugs on the drop table in the kitchen and was sitting, waiting, head bowed Quakerlike at the neck, the neck itself thin and white, a scar on the throat to the left of the windpipe, the shape of a nick you'd take out of an apple with a paring knife, a placid tow-head baby boy on her lap. All we get is boys around here, Elsbeth Jane saying. The mother waiting, head bowed, as though maybe Lenore would ax her, one fell swoop and spurting.

Downstairs in the kitchen, Lenore swallows a few more laxatives and moves the step stool over, to reach the box of Wagon Wheels behind the supply of bran cereal on the top shelf. When Darleen automatically placed her large hands, bright-red chipped nails, on her belly, Lenore momentarily had lost track of what she was saying, remembering what it was inside that nest of flesh, remembering what it had felt like to carry a baby and how Jack used to make love, when she was younger and thinner, and that made her recall what Elsbeth Jane had said one day, about her mum bringing something to school that the child had forgotten, about her mum "having to get out of bed anyway". Shame on her, but Lenore wondered at the time if all the woman did was lie in bed and drip, semen sticking to her thighs. If you thought about it, you could wonder at some of the things that child said.

She puts the box of Wagon Wheels on the table, finds the deck of cards in the utility drawer and sits down. But how Darleen and what's-his-name pulled off such a bright child is a mystery, because no matter what you said, all that mattered to them was that the child had been "sent back" to Grade Two, the only one in the whole class. About the child's father, the woman said, "His patience with her is run out. Whatever the girl's got and being slow-minded means the same to him." Lenore pictures the father, whom she's seen only from a distance in town one Saturday morning: beer-parlor belly, Levis saggy in the rump. "Well," she said, "Elsbeth Jane certainly does love her pigs."

What else was there to say? She had been exhausted, suddenly, with the effort of the day. Darleen smiled then, finally, and Lenore noticed a missing premolar on the right side, top; being married to Jack tended over the years to make her notice teeth. "Preacher says she has a real gift with animals." Darleen was pleased as a child. Even her cheeks turned pink.

Lord. Preacher, preacher. Shuffling the cards, she looks out the window at the big square plot of the summer garden. She had come up on a weekend in the spring, planted a garden, silly woman, trying to make the best of the move, and then in the chronic wetness everything rotted, rotted away, and the soil was wrong, too acid, too alkaline, too something. The snaky squash vines are black, muddy tangles, puny tomatoes bloated, beans hard. Maybe Elsbeth Jane would want to help her clean up, do some composting. Maybe the child – but no, that's silly, all that child cares about is pigs. Pigs and babies, cute and cuddly, hadn't she said that? Let Jack take some responsibility.

She brushes cookie crumbs off the table. To stretch the time it takes to play her three games of solitaire, she places the cards methodically, seven across, counting aloud. Then she flips through the deck three cards at a time, makes her hands move slowly. It crosses her mind about Jack and his office girl, Jennie what's-her-name, the new one, alone together all day. Why not.

Game lost, Lenore takes the cards up again. There was something sly about Darleen, she remembers now. One corner of her mouth twitched occasionally, as though she had secrets, or thought she had. Maybe just a tic, but maybe not. It was annoying, it annoyed her because it was as though the stupid twit had the nerve to imagine she actually knew something that Lenore herself didn't. Elsbeth Jane saying, pigs and babies, cute and cuddly. Elsbeth Jane saying, we keep getting boys around here.

When she picks up the cards again, her hands are shaking. She has her three games and puts the cards away. The day she's driven to 20 games in a row she'll know she's no longer coping. She takes the defrosted roast and the vegetables out of the refrigerator. Jack likes to eat promptly at 6:30.

The day's laxatives start to gurgle through her bowels.

She remembers Darleen and Elsbeth Jane in the doorway of the trailer, the woman's arm slack over the girl's shoulders. Both of them watching her. Waiting for her to leave.

The roast in the microwave, she goes upstairs to the bathroom, thinking of Darleen rooted to the steps of the trailer, her arm holding open the screen, her body leaning into it, relaxed, wearing the new, bright ruffly blouse, the man's Levis, the child climbing the steps toward her, being careful in her gumboots. Darleen looking at the girl, yes, Lenore recalls that now, the thin, scarred neck holding her fragile-looking head high but the eyes on the wispy-haired girl, the daughter, and she was beautiful, that was it, not flimsy or callow, the woman was beautiful, thighs thick in jeans too tight and her belly slightly swollen. Living in a man's world. Of smells and touch and bedsheets sweaty with careless lovemaking, the slim woman-body filling with gurgling babies, warm and smelling of baby powder and milk, babies evolving into placid, grinning tow-headed children, until the trailer bursts with them.

Lenore sits on the toilet and waits. Her bowels are burning, her belly cramps. She would like to close her eyes "real slow" like the heads of the geese, their decapitated bodies quietly gushing blood. It would be peaceful, to be behind those eyes closing on the light. She would like to sigh Lordy Lordy as her grandmother used to do, rocking in the dark. Just sit back and Lordy Lordy until the weight lifted from her heart.

On an Island

Whenever he stopped the car and climbed into the woods, even a short distance to take a piss, prickly branches reached out in ambush, to catch his hair or scratch his face. When he found a lake to wade in because the July sun scorched him through the windshield, its bottom gave way to muck, sucked at his ankles, muddied his last clean pair of khakis as he sloshed his way free. The views from the mountains made him dizzy, everything alive tried to sting or bite, and nobody was talking his language or talking much at all, at least to him. Two weeks of rattling along in his Volkswagen Beetle made Ronald hate British Columbia and its relentless scenery.

Now travelling south down the east coast of Vancouver Island, thinking of making his escape back to the States, he sees her there, around a bend at the edge of the road, standing still as an Indian, with a kid, about hip-high, by her side. She's about his age. He brakes and rolls down the window. She hardly blinks. She's wearing handmade hippie sandals and her feet are dirty.

Ronald is about to shift back into first when she says Howdy, in what sounds like a peculiar Southern accent, one he can't place but thinks he ought to. A fuzzy halo of black hair billows around her delicate, sunburnt face. She says, Will you ride us to the ferry?

Her eyes are a washed-out green, her nose is peeling and freckles spread across her cheeks. Her lips are full, but they're chapped, and she's wearing some kind of dusty coverall, baggy because she's thin except for her breasts which he can't help but notice, they're pressed down by the bib. On her upper arms are little reddish bumps. She has the kid clutched by the hand as though he'd get away, but to Ronald he doesn't look like he'd have the steam to get anywhere by himself. The kid, on closer inspection, is scabby-looking, with crusty, red-rimmed eyes. But then she smiles.

Hop in, he says.

As soon as she's settled in the car, she falls into a stupor that Ronald thinks could be from some dope she's on. The kid, washed out like a piece of wood discarded on a beach so that even his freckles look anemic, sucks three fingers, his hand turned palm up. They joggle along, a tight fit, in silence, her warm arm rubbing his. After a few miles she mutters something that sounds like Hungry, and he's about to say Pardon me? when she elbows him and points. She says she wants hot dogs and onion rings and Cokes from a cinder-block Mom 'n' Pop joint cut into the woods. What he knows and tries to tell her is that a cheeseburger and a glass of milk would be best for the kid.

Even at a distance while waiting in the car listening to her order what she set out for, Ronald thinks the way she talks is funny, a speech defect maybe, but there's something almost sweet about it. He looks up and she's back, shrugging and blinking, eyes to the ground. Oh, he says, reaching into his pocket for his wallet. How much? She shrugs again and he follows her to the take-out window. Impulsively he orders a cheese dog for himself, and a vanilla milk shake. How much? he asks the fellow and pays, although he wished he'd double-checked the prices with those on the plastic sign beside the window. He asks for a cup of water. The girl reaches for the bags, but he shakes his head at her, extracts a thick wad of napkins from the dispenser. They may as well take it easy, spread out at one of the picnic tables in the shade.

At the table the kid's mouth hangs open in a peg-toothed grin of anticipation. Hold your horses, guys, Ronald says to them. He folds the napkins five at a time and dips them into the water and swipes at the table. Dirty, he mouths, loud as though they were deaf or didn't speak English.

Slow down here, she says. It's right around the bend here.

Her "s" sounds are somehow lost. What she said was Nlow down here. Id right around the bend here. She sounds as though she has a cold. Or else she's dumb, which Ronald thinks is okay. The girls he knows at Northern Arizona University are always lording it over the guys, trying to sound smarter than they are. Acting superior, putting men down.

There's no ferry here, he says distinctly.

Is.

He slows. She points to a sign off in the trees. He says, You'd sure have to know where the darn thing is.

As they head down the dirt road, the kid, fingers in his mouth again and sound asleep, lets out a peeping noise, which makes the girl put a hand on his thigh. Ronald glances at her hand, small and pale, like Snow White's in the Disney movie. Except this one has a smear of ketchup and bits of relish on it.

At the end, there's a white-washed hut about twice the size of a telephone booth, a dock that's a makeshift raft with floating logs strapped underneath, and a tugboat tied to it, turquoise paint peeling on its wooden wheelhouse. The air smells of seaweed.

She turns to the kid whose forehead is beady with sweat. Wake up Baby Boy, hey Baby Boy. Ronald tries not to stare at her kissing the ugly kid's face.

The kid's eyes shoot open as though he's been branded. Wet fingers twitch out of his mouth. The girl lifts him onto her lap, crooning, Now BB, you be calm, no be worrying now. Mama's here. Mama's right here.

She looks at Ronald. Out of the blue she says, It doesn't matter what any of them say. He's mine.

What her speech sounds like is, Id dunt madder what any ovem mzay. He'd mine. The statement must be the conclusion of what she's been thinking about all along. She's been worried, Ronald sees now. He looks at Baby Boy. How old is he?

Six and some.

Is that his name? Baby Boy?

Nah, she says. His name is Rex. But Baby Boy, BB, suits him better.

Should I call him BB or Rex?

What's it to you?

I'm going with you, says Ronald. Where're you going?

He has to hurry to tuck a few clothes and toiletries into his backpack. Everything needs laundering, but he manages to find a dry washcloth, pajamas and an extra pair of socks before the boat, like something from a cartoon, gives a series of toots. For a second, struggling with his backpack, he thinks he's lost her. Then he sees her and the kid come splashing toward the boat. The girl swings BB up to some bearded weirdo on deck. Then she's calling. For him. Hey! hey! Ronald is suddenly so excited he almost forgets to lock the Volks. He just makes the boat, a flying leap.

His old man ought to see him now, taking off with a strange girl to God knows where. Being a conservative, his father wouldn't necessarily approve of her looks, but even he would look twice. He'd call her stacked. Ronald wrote a postcard from Calgary, to his mom: Sorry I lost my temper. He knows his mom got in trouble because of him, but it seems pointless, as the tug leaves the sheltered cove and a cold spray of ocean mists his face and neck, to have bothered mailing it. The old man is probably still out for his blood. He didn't mean working with your hands for a living was low class; what he meant was he personally was no good at drywall, he was allergic to the plaster that dried under his fingernails, causing his finger tips to burn. On the flagstone steps of their new tract house, his mom, small and resigned, with a helpless look in her eyes that always made Ronald's heart feel wrung out, said nothing to him, not then. Then his father turned from Ronald to her. Missus, you're the one raised him. Without moving toward her, he snapped his fingers, which made her scoot inside. He locked the door in Ronald's face.

At the stern where he finds the others, the guys are hairy, beards and ponytails, and the girls wear long granny dresses or else ragged Bermuda shorts, or less, displaying strong tanned legs. He hangs around a minute, listening to pieces of stories about Victoria and the mainland, before ducking below deck. There's room for about twelve passengers but only one is there, a grey-haired lady dealing Tarot cards on the bench beside her. He asks her the name of the island they're heading for, but whatever she says is lost over the cranking of the diesel engine as the tug bucks in the waves of Georgia Strait.

Ronald gives up trying to nap. The diesel smell swirling through the open doors is powerful and he keeps thinking about the girl, whatever her name is. He wonders if those bumps on her arm might mean ringworm. He wonders, studying his shirt sleeve with a frown, if ringworm can pass through a blend of polyester and cotton, remembering how her arm pressed against his in the car and how, too, even their hands touched sharing french fries. For that matter, she might have lice and her hair probably touched his, too. He sits up straighter, gives his head a furtive scratch. He can see BB on a stool up in the wheelhouse, next to an old man wearing a captain's hat that looks like it came from a variety store. Ronald performs elaborate yawns and stretches, for the benefit of the Tarot lady, just in case she's been watching him. He doesn't want her to think him strange.

In the wheelhouse he saunters back and forth, peering into BB's scalp, looking for crawling black things. His bowels start gurgling.

The girl appears from nowhere. She says, Your face looks halfway to the ground. Her clothes are wet and clinging; her hair is fluffing as it dries. She smells of the ocean.

He flinches when she touches his arm. What's your name? he asks.

Mory. Come on, BB. Come on out.

Where are we going? he blurts.

Home. There's a surprise outside, BB. You come now. She gathers him off the stool and steps into the cloudy sunshine.

To what island, please? Ronald asks again, but she doesn't hear, doesn't answer anyway, and exasperated, he tags after her, holding the rail as the tug churns through a sudden chop. At the stern, everyone is talking and giggling and digging into a cardboard box full of Bing cherries, tossing the bad ones into the wake and feeding good ones to each other.

Look what I got, she says. She opens her palm and reveals three dark and glowing Bings. She sticks out her tongue to show him how red it is. There's lots. Here Baby Boy, she says to BB, popping one into his mouth. Open up, she says to Ronald.

He knows the cherries ought to be washed, but they fill his mouth with sweetness. For a moment the sun comes out and bathes the boat in light that dances on the shiny sea swelling around them. Cherry juice drips off Ronald's chin. He forgets how he felt, locked out and with his useless fist raised, shouting loud enough the neighbors could hear, You leave my mother alone. He forgets about ringworm.

Although Canadians seem to have plenty of trees, Ronald guesses they must be saving them for something else; their toilet paper is stiff and thin, the kind that might be found in the Third World. The outhouse he's in, in the woods behind the dockside cafe, is smelly, but not as bad as some he's encountered on this trip. His diarrhea, almost a daily occurrence, he attributes to the foreign water. Before he had to make a run for it, he did manage to glance at the ferry schedule, and there wasn't one back until the day after next. It crosses his mind, head in his hands, bottom hanging over the boards, to wonder what he will do if she doesn't wait. He's sure there are no motels on the island.

On a search for her, he checks the cafe, open for food only on Friday and Saturday evenings, coffee and sweets in the afternoons; the store, about as big as his mom's new kitchen; the boat. Eventually he finds her and the kid, faces turned to what's left of the sun, lying in a bank of weeds beside the main road, paved for only a short stretch before it turns into gravel. Their clothes are wrinkled but dry, and the kid looks scrubbed. She opens her eyes and says, You and cherries don't agree I figure.

He chooses not to enlighten her about the elementary facts of digestion; it's been embarrassing enough. He has his pack shouldered, ready to head out. Where to? he wants to know. What he needs is a bath and some sleep.

Oh, pretty soon, she says.

What do you mean, pretty soon? What's happening? He tries one he heard on the ferry: What's going down? He shifts position, discovers his legs are weak. Well? She looks like she's gone to sleep. Well?

Sun's still out, she says. Rest yourself.

BB blinks pale eyes at him.

Ronald exhales, sits. Does he talk?

Only when he got something to say, she says and laughs. Baby Boy, you got anything to say?

BB shakes his head and grins his peg-toothed grin.

Ronald stretches out on the dusty weeds and sighs. He'll take a bath, do a wash when they get to her place.

You hungry?

He sits up on his elbows; he's been sound asleep. The sun is setting. She's on her knees smiling at him, her face and halo of hair close, blocking the orange wash in the sky. That fuzz would tickle his neck if she were an inch closer.

Mama?

He forgot about Junior Chapped Cheeks. He says, The kid talks.

He's hungry. There's a store here, connected up to the restaurant.

Connected, Ronald says, suddenly irritable. Not "connected up."

Connected. She taps his cheek twice with the tip of a finger before he can pull away. You hungry? she asks again. You got any money?

She buys heavy on carbohydrates and junk while the kid follows her around, stuffing his face with Wonder bread. Ronald's asshole burns.

He waits by the cash register not caring what she buys, as long as they get a move on. The bill almost cleans him out of cash.

She hitches a ride for them in the back of a 2x4. They squat in the truck bed, jolting along, heads down to avoid the wind and flying gravel, holding tight to grocery sacks. The road cuts through the forest of larch and cedar, with occasional clearings. When they climb out, in the middle of nowhere as far as he can tell, Ronald lurches, the ground still rushing by. She leaves behind one of the bags.

He starts to protest.

I owed, she says.

He looks first at BB, then at her. Her little knob of a chin is raised, but she doesn't meet his eye. And BB, wizened and passive beside her, reminds him of a kid in a book of photographs of poor southern people that his first-and-only girlfriend used to pore over. His heart is sinking at what he's got himself into.

Eat this, she says, unwrapping a Twinkie. For reasons of principle he hasn't had a Twinkie in years. His stomach growls. He goes ahead, opens his mouth and bites into the sugary cake.

From the woods BB produces a large, old-fashioned wooden slat wagon with chipped red paint and mismatched wheels. She loads the bags. While she pulls the wagon along ruts of a narrow road, more like a trail, winding into dense, ferny woods, BB scampers behind to keep the bags from toppling out. The two of them start singing. In the cowboy boots he's breaking in, bought at the Calgary Stampede, Ronald hobbles at the rear. Sometime after dark, he is at the end of nowhere, gawking at an enormous teepee perched on the edge of a cliff, the ocean directly below, stars overhead and pine needles under his blistered, burning feet. No house, no shack. No washing machine, no bath. A small black dog is snarling around his ankles.

When he wakes on a foamy on the board floor, the stove fire is crackling, the teepee is warm and smells of garlic and toast, and the light from an oil lamp glows on her face. She's knitting; at her feet, BB plays with the dog. When she sees he's awake she stares at him, her eyes dark and glittery. Now? she says and he's not sure what she means, although his penis seems to get a message. He rolls over on himself, feels the tingle of a blush rising up the back of his neck. Is it time to eat? His voice breaks. When he peeks at her again, one corner of the coverall is unbuttoned, and through the sheer fabric of her blouse he can see a dark nipple.

I'm starved, he says, looking away.

It's all right about BB, he don't understand.

Ronald clears his throat. Pushing the comforter back and adjusting himself, he gets to his feet. He has no intention of doing anything with her. The very idea, a kid watching, turns his stomach. No, he says. As soon as he's spoken, he wonders if he's gone and jumped to the wrong conclusion. He stutters, I mean no, to whatever you were meaning. Anything to eat?

Yep. Melted cheeses. You sure?

Sure of what?

She shrugs. BB, you come now.

Ronald has already started toward the compact wood stove, where a pot of spicy beans is bubbling, when he catches them, what they're doing, out of the corner of his eye. Her blouse is unbuttoned all the way. She takes a heavy breast in her hand and places the dark nipple in BB's open mouth. Holy smokes, he exclaims. He can't help but notice that her nipple is long and roughened, as though it's been sucked on a long time.

He scoops up a hot sandwich from the frying pan and ducks through the flap, to the clear air outside, dizzy with what he's seen. He burns his mouth cramming in runny Cheez-Whiz and white toast. At his grandma and grandpa's place in Texas, they used to eat Cheez-Whiz and homemade white bread with the crusts cut off and a dab of relish in the middle, "for fancy", his grandma would say. She was big-boned, like his old man, big work-red hands that did what they wanted, and not gently either; he remembers the times she washed his face practically raw. He glares at the glinting, sharp-edged stars through the dark spikes of trees. It's ignorant and pretty darn disgusting what she's doing in there.

Despite himself, staring at her nipple slick with the kid's saliva, his chest tightens. I came back for more, he says and flushes, realizing what she might think.

She prods BB with a knitting needle. You go on. Go on behind the curtain. Stay there now. Til Mama tells you. Take the dog. To Ronald she says, It's okay. He don't understand.

This isn't what he had in mind when he came back in. He intended to put an arm around her shoulders and sit quietly by her side, and together they would listen to the busy little poppings from the stove while he explained some facts to her, about right and wrong.

It's okay now, she says again and grins.

His chest is so tight all he can do is shake his head.

She says, You can though, eh? and steps out of the coveralls. She's not wearing anything underneath. Her bush is as thick as the forest he walked through. He starts to ache and tremble.

Afterwards, she wipes herself on a towel, pecks him on the forehead as his mom used to do before he went off to school. She dresses, gives the pot a stir and humming, adds kindling to the stove. He sits in the canvas sling chair and studies BB, rolling the ball along a path set with wood scraps, giggling deep in his throat. The pale eyes under the long lashes blink slower than what might be normal. Something must be wrong with this kid, with his mind maybe. A real out-of-institution retarded kid. And her, serving beans and slices of cheese into bowls, she has something wrong with her speech. He remembers that he didn't use a rubber. He doesn't even have one on him.

Mory. He says her name. Would you come here, please? She puts down the wooden spoon and comes over, sits on her haunches in front of him, folding the skirt she's put on between her legs.

Are you protected?

Protected?

Ronald clears his throat. You don't really want a baby, do you?

No. She's smiling. Her eyes crinkle. Don't fret, she says. I already got the one baby I intend to get.

Ronald frowns. Is he all right?

She looks over her shoulder. He looks all right to me.

That isn't what I mean. I mean –

He looks all right to me. He's been tested. He don't even have to go to school. Ya hungry? She rocks on her heels and gives him a fierce look before retreating to the crate that's being used as a table.

What I mean is, is he retarded? Do I need to explain it?

Get on outside, she says, standing over him waving the dripping spoon. You got a big mouth. Move.

At the edge of the clearing beside the wood pile, she stops. You got a big mouth on you.

I have a right to know, he says, taking her arm.

You got the right to exactly nothing. Some things are your business. Like this – she gestures to her breasts, her crotch – I gave you. I owed. The rest is not your business.

His cheeks smart. He catches his breath. Prickles start up the back of his neck as he says, keeping his voice even, Why do you let him do that, him being so old? He narrows his eyes, surveys her figure silhouetted against the glow of the kerosene lamps from the teepee. From the first time she smiled, the way she begged money, his father would have recognized her for the bitch she is.

She's saying, I don't know you any time at all, eh? I know BB a long time. Everybody else gets some, why not him? She turns again, to start back. Let go of me.

He almost lets her go, but then his grip tightens so that he can feel the gristle and bone beneath the flesh. She shrugs in an attempt to free herself and he yanks her back, his breathing suddenly loud, he hears it, rasping, and sees her eyes widen in surprise. Hold your horses, he says. I have something for you.

I bet. Forget it. I paid.

But she's watching him, wary, even as she tries to pull her arm away. He clasps his fingers around her throat, fits his thumb into the soft indentation. Through it her pulse is strong and fast, her heart is racing. He continues to press, until she's breathing out of a mouth gone slack. His body has begun trembling, his balls ache. He touches the long, teat-shaped nipples through her peasant blouse, plays with them, and releases his hold. Now stand still, he says. Please.

Sometime in the night a dog barks in the distance and he half-wakens, smells the dead cooking fire, hears the little black mongrel snoring close enough to touch. He wants to make love to her, nice this time, but when he raises himself over her, he sees BB sleeping on her other side.

Later he wakes sweaty and out of sorts. He pulls on his pants and finds them sitting around a small fire even though the sun is bright. The dog has his head on his paws. The air smells of sausages and sea.

Howdy, she says in greeting.

Howdy, says BB.

The dog nips at his pant leg. He shoves it away with his foot.

Do you have any Cheerios?

Cheerios?

Cheerios. You know, little round oat things. Cheerios. He's gritting his teeth.

Why you want them?

I like Cheerios for my breakfast, he says. It's what I prefer.

Sure.

Where are they? I would like them, please.

We got Fruit Loops. Don't we, BB? Got Fruit Loops?

I don't want that crap.

Oh. We don't got Cheerios.

Do they sell Cheerios at the store? he asks.

At the store?

Do they sell them there at the store?

Sure, why not?

He inspects her face. There is a look about her eyes in this light that he recognizes. Her pale green eyes are sunken and bruised. She uses her shirt sleeve to dry her face. Her answers have tried to please him and now he's made her cry. Sure, why not? she said. His center of gravity shifts. If he snaps his fingers, she will scurry.

Crosslegged and silent on the blanket he methodically eats the sausages and overcooked fried eggs. He sets his plate on the ground and looks meaningfully at her breasts. Now I'm a tad thirsty. To BB he says, Go inside. Behind the curtain. Until I tell you to come out.

Her eyes are glistening, watching BB do what he's told. She crawls over to where Ronald sits. On her knees, she raises her shift and holds out a breast to him. Ronald opens his mouth, tongue flat. The sun warms his face and the closed lids of his eyes.

She says, Don't you talk rude to that child. That's my child, and shoves his chin away, making a move to rise. He grabs the edge of her shift, pulling her over and pinning her down. A deep wailing from her fills his ears as he presses her shoulders into the dirt. He grins into her flat little face. He feels himself turned on by her struggles, he's stirring and growing. Then her knee jabs him in the balls and the pain, sharp as lightning behind his eyes, throws him off balance. He cries out, rolls onto his side, knees pulled to his chest. What he hears in his head is his mom, the night he was furiously packing. How could you, Ronnie, hurt him so? hissed in passing in the upstairs hall.

Later, when they see him approaching the beach, they run from the half-moon of sand and duck under the waves and swim out. He has twisted his ankle on the steep path down and it throbs. They are naked, glistening as seals on an outcrop of rock in the bay. Arms around their knees, they stare at him silently, like two wild animals. They are so still, if he didn't know they were there he wouldn't notice them.

He squats next to their castle structures, mussel and clam shells stuck in wet sand, with pebbles piled in pyramids. Shifting his weight onto his good foot, he adds a clump of moss to a clumsily formed turret. He fingers her clothes, her stained flower-print shift, her bikini panties. He picks them up. Shouting out to her on her silly rock would be demeaning. He'll wait her out.

In the teepee he sniffs himself. He stinks like an animal, his smell is mingling with old garlic and stale wood smoke. His swollen ankle aches. He could lie in wait for her here, on the foamy. Or he could rest and go back down to the beach and simply by his presence force her to stay on that rock until her tits turned blue. He could sit there on the crescent of sand, wearing a sweater he's bound to find, eating the Twinkies he paid for. He could sit on the sand, arms hugging his knees, and watch her and the kid slowly drown, the tide rising inch by inch, higher and higher, to her ankles, her calves, her crotch. He sits up. He has nothing to beg forgiveness for.

Among her belongings, he finds what he expected: men's clothes, jeans, T-shirts, underwear, an assortment of leather fringed hats and a leather jacket that's too big for him, with a torn shoulder seam. A sweater a moth has eaten holes in. He begins throwing kindling from the basket, canned food from the open shelves, the kid's toys; piece by piece he starts to rip her clothes.

He doesn't know what it is the bitch wants, what any of them want. What he wants is to smash her smug face. He wants her on her back, turned on and begging, tasting of dirt and wind.

Embers

Like a stiff fetus the old woman lies curled under the quilt in her faded paisley dress, her brown woollen stockings unravelling at the thigh. On her feet are ankle-high shoes, the laces untied, the leather sooty black, soft and thin as worn velvet, molded around bunions and quarter-moon toes, whose nails are thick and yellowed as ivories on an old piano.

Lying on her side, she can see through the dining room directly into the kitchen, to one corner of the enamel gas stove, under the open window hung with a white eyelet curtain. On the stove is a faded orange and white shoebox, its sides softened, lolling outwards. For some time she has tended its contents, fussed shreds of newspapers and bits of cloth into a miniature resting place.

Her tongue flicks across chapped lips. The quilt is heavy, weighs her down, like the lake water and storm clouds in the dream; the shoes she can't remove are anchors. Her name is Mattie, and she must get up. The bossy voice of that girl who comes to lord her youth over her, flush her toilet, put cheese on her crackers, crank up the kettle, has told her: If you don't get up, they'll take you away. So she must. And if you wet your bed again, Mother will misplace you. Put you someplace. Mother says you must not forget and wet yourself.

Mattie has responsibilities for the precious life, Lord, in the shoebox. Sitting, she teeters on the edge of the bed like a kewpie doll at the back of the clown-mouth throw booth in the fairground, where Colm once took her, courting her against her father's wishes. Colm was a devil, that one, in top hat and tails. And sweet as molasses on sourdough pancakes of a Sunday morning. Oh, sweet as fresh maple dissolving down an open throat.

Mattie is aware of her feet hanging heavy and wonders through how many sunrises she forgot to get up, forgot to eat; how many times daylight hit the pocket-sized mirror hanging from a string on the wall across the room, that she put there herself in order to keep track of when to rise, when to shine. Rise and shine with the sun, her father taught, and owe no man. But light is hard to see when you're this damn old and your eyes themselves are a sight, filmy and fading, milky, running and awful. As a nurse, she used to hate the eyes of the old, but her eyesight's too poor now to look at her own except up close, peering into the mirror. She's better at seeing distance. Which is good and bad, both. How many mornings has she been faraway, busy with the dream, forgetting to get up?

If the Welfare'd send that damn girl more than a few times a week, you wouldn't be in this pickle. It's a shame, all right, the foolish things age makes you do. Get up with the moon by mistake, start fussing with tea in the dark, think you've gone plumb blind and all it is, the middle of the night. Lets the dream of what happened on the island catch you awake and you crust up your eyes with weeping and then scratch at your face just to blink, to see Jesus thumbtacked at the foot of the bed, Jesus with his blue eyes and light brown hair, your Saviour, Mother said and Oh, you did need saving from that devil man who took you.

Shame floods Mattie's face, the same as being out of doors and looking down, finding the thick black laces snapping around her ankles, untied, again, the heat in her cheeks driving her bowed and muttering home.

Today she won't be caught out like a damn fool. She's already spied the shoes dangling at the end of her body; she's already fixed attention on the laces. First you have to get off the bed, go find the damn chair, bump into it more likely, sit, lift one foot up on the footstool and get to work. Then the other. Do the other shoe, too.

The shoe business takes time. Blood rushes to her head. Mattie is tickled there is blood left in her vines – she thought vines instead of veins, veins, Mattie, you were a nurse – and when she is finished tying the laces she stands, holds the back of the chair, stands with her shoulders back. Her supervisors always said, Now there's good posture. Follow Mathilda's example, girls.

In the kitchen, she mills from counter to sink until she remembers the shoebox and her responsibility. The box is a man's, one of her husbands'. She lowers herself onto the stool in front of the stove. Colm, the devil. Or blind Howard. Old man with liver-spot hands mercifully kept to himself.

But there's a draft, the curtain flaps. Air cold as snow hits her knuckles as she stands, clutching the window sill. Her dog Spotty will be in the yard waiting for a scrap of something for herself and her little pups. She must shut the window. Her baby must not catch a chill. There is so much to do. She must shut the window against the wind, she must eat, and where is Spotty? Spotty has got away again, bad dog. She must go looking for Spotty, bad dog.

She pokes her finger into the box. No bad smelling pup there now, awful thing, the way it did not get up – and after she took care of it, stroked it, finger-fed it milk and soaked bread and loved it, runt of a thing, when she took it still pink from Spotty's teat. It turned nasty. The girl with the bossy voice said mean things. But it was the pup's fault. The bad pup had made her lose control, had made her weep.

The dollbaby nestled there now is good. Eyes blue and clear. Smiling. Belly button neat and flat. Other parts in a clean diaper. But the pink skin is cold and Mother must do something.

She digs in a drawer under the counter, finds a paper napkin. She pets the sweet baby, her own sweet baby. Her fingers return to the drawer, scrabble against peeling drawer paper. She finds a cracker, eats it, crumbs in the crevices of her dry lips. In the cupboard is a box of crackers, the box red, she recalls that it is red and on the table against the far wall is margarine in a bowl but she must slow down, she must not fall and break her hip like old women do. But it is exciting to remember, to eat, to lift the knife greasy with the smell of food to her lips to lick clean, to dig into the mound of soft margarine in its yellow container and eat the red crackers. The crackers are not red, Mattie. The crackers are whitish, with dents in them. Eat. Sweet.

She sits at the table, brushes her face with the hem of her skirt. Spotty should be barking for food, damn old bitch with her crotch spread to the world and legs on her would jump any fence when she wants it. Damn old bitch. A dog, blind Howard used to say. It's just a dog Mattie, is all. Don't know no better. Let her have her way, Mattie. It's nature.

It ain't nature, you fool. It's the devil has hold of her, dog or no dog.

She imitates his poor grammar, using "ain't" to taunt him but he doesn't hear the rightness or wrongness, isn't educated. Just a young hick farm boy who got himself in a war.

When Howard didn't need her or if he wanted to play hymns on the piano she would sit him down and then march out of the house and collar Spotty, drag her home, lock her in the yard again, slap her on her nose so that her teats, pathetic and lean and still hanging from nursing the pups that Mattie drowned in the toilet, would jiggle. Jiggling empty teats on a dog's belly. Mattie's own teats aching, once. Awful. Put it out of mind.

Find Spotty, bring her home.

Out on the road, wearing her black coat. Pocket is torn and hanging, but it is a nice coat, someone said so. Some man gave her the money for it. Blind Howard, who liked the curly-sheep feel of it. Like your hair used to be, he said, before you cut it off, all permanented and pretty in my hands. She was his nurse. It was her job to be permanented and pretty. In 1942 he was a paralyzed soldier. She hears him at the card table talking to cronies: Paralyzed in '42, he would say, my legs and all but not there, you know, not there, he'd say, nodding at the V in his lap, my wife'd tell you the trouble I give her with *that*. And smirk and wink at her and the fellows would laugh and wink at her. They still knew what it was like to stab a woman. Blind Howard with his Braille cards lied.

Men lied. That was nature, she would liked to have said to Howard. And wanting girls. *That* was nature, if you were looking for a definition of sin.

She presses her palms to the coat. She must not think of sins. Howard was dead from the waist down. She married him and took care of him until the rest of him died, and that was what mattered.

A rock hits her foot.

"Spotty? Spotty dog?" To her ear her unused voice grates, like pebbles under water when her boat glided toward the island's beach. But she is not in the dream; she is awake and outside, wearing a coat. She says, "Spotty? You come home now, bad dog." A child is snickering from behind a hedge.

"You're crazy," the voice pipes. "Dumb dog's dead, crazy old lady." A splatter of gravel hits her shoes, tinkly as rice they threw at her wedding to the devil. Stinging her face with the truth she should have known. Should have known that if he'd take her, a child of fifteen, he'd take anybody, bring her sickness, turn her female mucous yellow with disease.

"Child," she says. "Do I know you?"

She squints, sees only a blue baseball cap and eyes that she can't make out clearly in the darkness of the day, clouds overhead blotting the sun. And then the child is running, away from her groping hand as she stumps toward the hedge. The child is running and shrieking. She isn't drooling is she? She is dressed, isn't she?

Shame. Cheeks wet. Making a spectacle of herself. Who wouldn't run, an old woman in black, circling herself. Shame: heat, hot blood. Clotted on white sterile rags, red turning black, exposed to air. Something important lost for good, like Spotty is lost for good, and Howard is lost for good, and Colm, damn his soul, is lost for good. Oh, Mother. You didn't tell me how it would hurt when he came at me, again and again. Oh, Mother, you didn't tell me how he would fill my mouth with shame.

The running child flees heavenward, out of her sight, soars above the trees of the island where the boat slipped onto pebbles into the shore of her decision, solemn in the wind and moonlight where something bad was dug from within her. But it is a child soaring away out of sight leaving her in a nest of leaves while it rises above the forest. Father said, Owe no man.

Inside, she pets the shoebox baby, picks at its coverlets. The napkin covers the smiling, blue-eyed, eyelashed face. Babies are not to be buried. Hers is still cold in its little bed and its Mother must do something.

Her hands hurt from tugging at the window, which won't close. In the other room, she unties the shoelaces to ease the pain and climbs into bed, shivers into the dream waiting in her place under the quilt.

A branch from the sycamore pushes against the house with the will of a memory knocking. Something wanting to get in, carried by the wind whipping up outside. The dream: A rowboat in the middle of a lake, water lapping at its sides, the lake ruffled. The girl rowing is stubborn, works against an easterly breeze. She rows the boat out from the shore with the strength of her will, toward the small island where the tree tops are bending, rustling in the beginnings of a storm. It is dark in the forest on the other side. Mattie both watches from the shore and rows and is afraid for them both. The rower is seventeen and married a year to the man Colm. Mother says her duty is to her husband. Mother says, You made your bed, now lie in it.

Mattie says, Mother, I did. You let me have him sweet in my arms at first and then he wanted too much and I couldn't wring the sheets clean enough. My belly is filled with his germs, Mother. I saw them in a book. They are black wiggling things.

In her bed, Mattie moans.

The girl on the shore is simply sashed in a dress of her time, a peony-printed muslin she sewed on the new Singer he bought her, thinking, he said, to make her happy. The skirt is calf-length. She hemmed it by hand. It snaps at her legs, shows off her bare ankles and feet. The old woman dreaming roots the girl to the shore, buries her in muck to her knees so she is unable to walk the few steps toward the boat, oars at ready, in its hull rags white and clean (for even then she was tidy, she knew about cleanliness). The old woman wills that bitter girl to stay on shore, to stay and watch a simple storm come up. Let her cry a little, sigh and fold her arms across her belly as women do.

Mattie twitches. The wind cracks a branch against the side of the house. There is knocking, but the girl on the shore does not listen, her spirit so dark she doesn't consider. Doesn't wake up.

She insists on stepping into the boat. Balances herself, smoothes her skirt before she sits, she is fastidious, she will make a good nurse, and rows into twilight, into the coming storm. The girl in the boat doesn't know the old woman, has not dreamed her, has not conceived herself as old, the one left behind. Has not considered that her drama will run for decades under the surface of chores and daily talk. The old woman remembers very well: the moon, prying maternal eye, following her through the tangling trees blowing in the beginning of fury.

Mattie clenches her fists, digs sharp fingernails into her palms, falls again, against her wishes, into the nest of velvety forest soil, the top layer brushed aside with the girl's bare hands. She takes a goodly-sized branch and whittles it carefully with a knife from her kitchen and then matter-of-factly opens herself, places the whittled wood deep, drives it home, kills his thing growing in her. The branch is sharp, the surface blood is quick to rise, tender parts cut. She tears at the hidden fleshy parts he wants.

The thing itself is forced out onto the forest bed, a small mass of jellied head and tail, the eye looking inward, dying in moonlight. It has a miniscule bump, there, in that place. It would have been a son for him. She stuffs the rags into her bleeding before she faints. She is no good anymore, scarred and useless to him.

Mattie wakes. Her baby will be cold. She pushes herself up, reaches for the chair, trembling. She hears noises, rattlings, tappings. "Lord?"

Blinking, she looks for Him in the darkness and waits. "Lord?" She pulls the lamp chain, peers around the room. Her eyes find the picture at the foot of her bed. The man is young and handsome, with soft deer-coloured hair and beard and blue eyes clear and bright, a halo over his head. He looks serene and trustworthy. A nephew? An uncle as a young man? A son? Never a son.

The pebble-throwing child was afraid.

The wind buffets the house.

In the kitchen the curtain brushes her face as she tucks her baby in. Shame on her. She forgot about lighting the stove.

On the shelf she finds a box of wooden matches. She twists a knob, hears the hiss, strikes a match. She moves the shoebox close to the warmth, gropes back to bed, turns off the lamp.

She watches the blue light from the gas burner flicker to the rhythm of the wind, is watching when a sudden gust sweeps through the window, knocks the curtain rod loose. It clatters onto the stove. The curtain falls on the burner, flares. The shoebox ignites, blackens, curls in the flames. The baby cracks. Mattie sinks back, watching from the far shore, gratitude welling in her heart.

My Daghter

I lover her cheeks, her face, the fat across the back of her sholders
    when I am hugging her, I love her beatiful lips
    maybe wrong for her mother to feel
    but her lips are kissable even with the bubblegum clotting her
mouth and
    giving her that chipmuck munchy mumps look to one side of her . i
love her thighs
    that she wrap in saranwrap to thin them down and she
    laugh as she done it. after she done it, her laughter entering the
    livingroom umber with my TV shadows black and white, somber
TV
    shadowy over my face watching lifeless
    ly because i am tired from working all day
    in the laundry, my ankles swollen inside white socks bleached to
    stiffness.
    I love d her laughing at the saran wrap around her thighs, but then i
    bawled her out about the waste of money and the cream oozzing
out from

underneath it.

On sale for 1.29 for 30ft the saranwrap says, not so much after all but she is

gone from the room and i am back with my eyes closing and opening in front of

the TV andI am too tired to get up

That was my frist poem.

I am taking a class in the afternoon about typing and spelling when I can walk down there, to the communty center. When my legs are not acting up. I was trying to prove to my daghter by caring on about the price of saran wrap that we are truly needy. But with her in it, my life is not really as poverty stricken as it looks. But she had been to see her daddy, and boy he can do for her what I can't, and she is always bragging out about it, the jeans he bought her, the stake he fed her. JHe dont want to keep her, though, and this she dont' know of. Nor need to.

Sometimes I want a baby, I want that little baby I see somektimes with the spiky black hair and the face that looks just like my baby's

Oh, I want that baby so much that when I got on the elevator and the baby was there in one of those cary baskets and her father – oh, not handsome enough and with a pot belly to be the father of that perfect baby so like my own was – that my longing showed out of my eyes. I know it did. Just shot out of my eyes like bullets. The mother of the baby saw it and moved closer to the baby. In the elevator was the thought that someone could kinnap the baby. There was only the mother, the father, the baby;'s brother along with her on the upward ride. So it would be me, the one to kinnap her. So I shrugged and stared at a writing on the evelator wall, something my daughter probably wrote, most likely, just like her.

I don't remember things like the TV storys I saw last month, they're gone from my mind. I wonder about that disease, olztimers, it seems popular and then I remember how much popularety I've managed to get hold of so far, and breath a sigh of relief.

I am not a leader in anything, although once I was asked to leave school because I said hell and was a bad influense on the other little boys and girls. And when I went to Sunday school those few times, my arms was streaked with dirt. Now can I really be only a hardluck case when I am able to say it about myself? Or when anybody looks at me, am I in their mind supposed to be stupid, but lovable? a hardluck case, her daghter and her, the two of them hillbillys, dusty but lovable and smoking cigarettes at the table in their greasy-spoon kitchen eating cornpone with their neighbor, some weirder lady. This is what they see.

And There Are hillbilly things about me that makes me sad sommctines. My freckles.

Freckles make a person feel younger . And they make you feel poorer. Except for an actreess or two, rich people don't have freckles. Mine are peppered on me, not dlibdelcately either, not the delcate little trail sprinkled across the nose. Mine are like a road, streaks at a distanse of a few feet. Big as peppercorns.

At least they are fading with years. But then so is my carrotty hair but then so are my eyes.

We have a neighbor lady who lives in the long ago past, and she wears a sad, black coat kind of threadbare like you read in fairytailes soemtimes and she has a little boy that she takes care of from her daughter. He's a illegitmate, makes the granny sad, I reckon. But she don't much love that child though there's nothing wrong with him that I can tell. The daghter just took off on her and left the boy behind.

This lady says stuff like "So whars her uther child? She had anuthr wone you know and she give it away real young, so whars it? Tthat wone woulda been best, not like this awfull stupid wone."

I wrote it terrible so you could picture how she talks. Pretty bad.

The lady's real thin,, skinny as a chicken bone sucked clean by a coyote. (I just made that coyote business up, figuring it sounded hillbilly but I have never saw one myself.) Anyhow, I seen the neighbor lady in the grocery store with the child and he's just smiling round nice, petting this, that, other things, nice and smileying. And she's meanfaced like a witch all uglyfaced. Poorr chiled. He never did anything bad but get born. She never talks to him, never says a word and so he don't speak that I heard. After the store she's carrying her sacks and he's rubbing his hands along a wire fence and she stops in the park and stands there. Just like a staduu, no moving, watching down at her sacks in the grass and the boy is flying with his arms out, a airplaine. Hes smiley too so I guess she takes care of him allright. Her missing daghter obviously don't like him either.

I went on the Welfare, legs being bad like they was, swollen big as church pillyers, blobs of freckles growing bigger too. Awful. What the heck I figure. This doctor, he'll sign anything, he don't care.

That round whirly thing in the park? What's it called?

My writing is improving. Iam leaning phonics and so can spell many more things and reconize my mistakes now. So far in this part there are 3 or more mistakes, probably. I didnt want to be to perfect or you wouldn't believe (i befor e) my story. You wouldn't keep on, to see what happens to me next.

Well! my girl comes home dancey daisy and says "Hey Ma" - she calls me Ma and I hate it - "we gonna have us a baby round here." Well, I will tell you, I am pissed right off! "Je-sus" I say and slap her face because she's talking Black, you know. Just because we live in Housing she comes up with this kind of talking and it pisses me right off! "So what color is this baby of ours going to be?"

Then, and about time, she starts snivling. I don't have to look in the mirrer to see my freckles are standing out like rocks on my face. I am writing slower now so it is easyer to read as I write and I can catch more m istakes but whn i start takingl baabout that girl it makes e stitter with shame and arage!

"So what color" I repeat myself.

"Mixed" she says.

"So even that baglady next door's daughter comes up with white babiys and my daghter makes them mixed?"

"But hers is dumb!" my daughter's yelling at me now.

"Not the first one," I remind her.

"That's only what that baglady says! We dont know for sure!"
Which is true. I am fairminded as a person can be. "Piss" is all I say.
"Je-sus. Keerrist. How come your so damn dumb?"

Then she starts in, her skin white under the zits, her eyes flashing
black as the nigger beby we're going to get round here. "It's all your
fault, Ma," she says "You always act too fine and hoitydoity and pay
me no mind like I'm a chield, well" She says "I'm not and now you
damwell know it. You always say I wasn't smart enough in school, I
couldn't get my letters right and I always got failing in spelling. Not
smart like you Ma" (and here she's being sassy) "So I went out up on
the roof like the song says and I let the blackboy do it to me Ma and
that's it!!!"

I can't believe I'm hearing what I'm hearing. I slapherface so hard
she backs up into the fridge and rocks it. My handprint is on her face. I
always wondered if that can happen. It's not the whole print, just the
fingers of it,. She shuts RIGHT UP and takes to sorry crying, which is
what she should of been doing all along.

Time goes by.

I have got dry skin on my hands, that comes from having freckles all
over. This dry skin seems to get worse when I worry as I am doing with
my dahgter growing bigger and eating Ripple Chips like a pig in front
of my eyes. I made her quit the smoking since I read about babyies
born small, so now she has to go outside to smoke, which unfortunately she does too often. I could smack her, she's so dumb, but she's
young. Heck. Was I so smart?

Today that little boy from the next apartment knocked on our
door. Tough kind of knockknocks stronger than I thought he would be
able. (He's only about four, his granny bothered to tell me one day). So
he knocks knocks and I open the door (my daghter is still sleeping, in
general she mostly sleeps) and he's standing there, round blue eyes just
gazing at me straight on. He don't move, just stand there gazing, and
finally after we look upon each other for a time, his finger lifts up and
points to where he lives next door and I reckon he's trying to tell me
something.

So I poke him to get him moving and then he leads me to his apartment where the baglady is lyinging in her bed, deader than a doormnail. She looks awful. Grey as paste left out in the air too long. She been sleeping in her coat poor thing and now this chiled starts to cry, pettin on her face. Tears roll down his thin cheeks smeared with dirt like my arms used to be in Sunday School. He crys with no sound. Just wet on his face, in streams not stopping. Then his nose starts running too and he is the stickyest person I have ever had to hold, next to a newly born babyie. He falls into my arms like he needs to be there. I haul him home.

When I get him to home I know I'm supposed to be calling somebody oficial on the phone. But his mamma is disapeared long ago and he's just small and hungry looking and when my duaghter drags herself up out of bed looking like a house, she's not so happy to see this drippy kid at first, but I talker into it. He's harmless enough. He just sits at the table cramming in the Wheatees with his hands sort of bothering with the spoon not very frequent and milk slopping all over his chin and the table. He is a pityful sight. But he's a childe. And my dahgter, something goes on with her all off a sudden, some light hits her eyes, starts a fire inside.

Let's take him to the park, she says. I think he needs the air.

So we do. We place him between us hand in each hand and we lift him down the curb like my daddy and mamma used to do me (and my daghter never had her dad and me together long enough for us to do that for her,) but her and me, she and I we do it for this little child,. He lifts his legs automatic when we hoist him and I think he's okay, he knows what to do. My daughter has got tomatoe sauce on her pregnant shirt but I don't even care.

In the park we go right for the whirlything, whatchucallit, that goes round and you have to jump on it but first get some body to help you make it go. Then we all jumped on. And that's how we came to get this orphand boy and take care of him. He's no trouble at all. Thats what the story was about in the first place. Love and babyies.

✳
More

What happened is. We get the boy settled in fine and dandy and my daghter has got her little one well born, when on an afternoon she comes running through the door, huffiing and puffying into the apt. crying out, "There's a girl over the park needs us."

I am babysitting with Joyann, my daghter's five months-old, who is our joy for sure. She has got the whiteness on the souls of her feet and her hands and her hair is springy and her eyes are the widest brown ones, so you would know she is a Black person's baby as well as ours. But we are the ones have got her out of my daghter's own body and the boy who did it with her has probably forgot and we say okay about that, fine and dandy. Joyann sparks, is why. She has got genuine joy down so deep that looking into her eyes makes you capsize a while, then you come back out laughing and leaping . In your heart.

"Where is Roger?" I want to know. We think that's the name he was saying was his. His tongue is thick, and his granny was right about him, what she said about him being dumb, but what can he do about it? Is it his fault he was born dumb? Should we just toss him like old pototoe chip bag into the garbage because Creation has made him dumb? And why was that, anyway? Because, how I see it, this (bad word) daghther of our dead neighbor lady was drinking and taking drugs, most likely was it. Now who is to blame there is a chjile here standing in my kitchen drooling sometimes and other times smileying to beat the band? He is in the flesh, he has got eyes in his head that see out, his skin burns if he puts it on the radiator as he sometimes does, forgetting what we told him, he cryies with sounds you would not want to hear outside a zoo in the lonelyiest of his nights when I think he is remembering his mama and how she left him for the old lady granny to raise up. He is more than meets the eye and somehow less too,.

So, "Where is Roger?" I ask my daghter.

"He's over the park with this one I am telling you about, he is guarding her so she don't run off, she's in a bad way, she needs us."

Says she "needs us" and I am happy because it means my daghter is gaining sensibilivies what I didn't reckon she had. At least she is growing into them, and mmm, for a minute while I am standing by the stove, her one Joyann in my free arm and stirring pea soup with the other, I feel satisfied with the way of the world.

Joyann on my hip, gurgling and flapping her arms like wings, I go chugging down the stairs clumpy as a house in my raggedy looking slippers I ought to know better than to wear in public, but. My daghter is in a state of some kind over a stranger in the park and Roger shouldn't be left by himself a second, he is liable to come to harm.

I am taking now at the Center a hist. class in American hist along with English, basic II. The class has set me thinking and I have thought up a theory about what the south is. I started expressing this theory in class and the history teacher took to smiling, which for some is bad, they get dander up, and to me, is not. When she is smileying my way, there is in her uptown face a glowingness that I feel, like from a plug-in heater. She is not grinning badly, she is offering me courage, and so here it is.

The south (South) is the root of America, because everybody comes from there at one time or another, except for the families of the Pilgirms who just stayed in Boston and never felt the need to leave because they were first there and everybody else who came along was basically a strange newcomer, forever. People went to the South, white people to get land and Black ones dragged there against their wills, and then childern grew up, left, scattered up and out, like a fan a lady on a balcony somewhere would wave. The craziness in Califonria is not much compared to the South, where Klans come from, where Bible Belters started their preaching, where jazz begun and different modes of speaking the Kings English also. And folk singing, too, all those Irish in hollows twanging awry. In the South they got not much education there and lots of poverty, I should know. Big holes in the ground, Mines and bosses too.

To get the South out of you takes more time then you usually get. It will take past my daghter and I don't know about Joyann, being part

Black. Being in Housing keeps you in a Limbo but I don't know what else they could do with us, because.?

Getting the South out is watching ducks fly without wanting to shoot them or watching baby pull pans from the cubboard and not wanting to slap it and call it bad. It is cleaning up after, yourself, even if you are plumb beat (this is what they say in the South, plumb beat). It is also spotting a racoon and not wanting to eat it.

Too many days pass where me and mine do nothing much is what I reckon is wrong with us. We cook and wash up and we clean a bit and we buy some groceries, what we can, and we play with the little ones, tickle them and take them to the park, and we do the washing and my dagter has even ironed a few things in her time. We watch the TV. Sometimes we read a romance, out loud back and forth, few pages at a time, but it is like waiting and I don't kmow how we are not the same as somebody like the hist. teacher except I know we are not, and I don't know what we are waiting for, either, until my daghter comes roaring through the door: "There's a girl in the park needs us" and maybe that's it.

Sitting in a canvas swing her long yellow hair mangy with unwashness, her head bowed down, she is twirling a little like Roger likes to do, scuffling her shoe in the dirt and studying it, the patterns of it on the ground. Roger is standing tall near her, keeping guard, bless his heart, just like my daghter told him to do, his eyes glued on her.

The blouse she is wearing is tattered a bit like she has fallen on the street or been drug along it. She has on a skirt that is too short and her legs, long thick ones, are striped with puddles of dirt that have dried up, leaving water marks on her skin. One shoe is flap-soled and both used to be black. She is a sorry sight about sixteen or so I reckon and looking like she has been through the wrong end of a washing machine,, in clean, out dirty.

Joyann is giving her google noise like a baby will do, but the girl she don't look up, acts like we're invisible to her. I have been invisible in my time, as a chield scared out of its wits, but I am too big, too old, too damn fat to put up with ignoring from a youngster needs a serious bathing. So I just slap my hand down in one of hers hanging lost on her lap and haul her up, giving Joyann to my dagther all in one swell swoop, and she comes along, wilting across the brown-color grass of this sadly treeless park next to the Housing, comes along head bowed down practically to her chest bone.

Up those stairs, elevator out again, up and me like a stuck pig in sweat, but already I am milling through my mind, With my household multiplying like rabbits me and my daghter have got to find better work than collecting the Welfare, and taking on schooling. Already I know this girl belongs to us, even as we undress her from her rotty, soiled clothes and one-leg her at a time into the tub. It's her foot touching the water that makes her eyes perk and she looks at us like we are going to hit her bad . She wenches her arms free of us and one foot in the tub and the other not, she closes her eyes and twists her body round, putting her dirtynailed hands on her girl hips and struts her hay-colored hair-parts out.

I am looking at her with my mouth wide open and my daghter is the same, only her eyes scared of she knows not what. And what it is, this big girl with eyebrows that go a mile is acting like we had a camera on her, she is waiting for the click. While we are standing pondering this through, she turns her body butt-end out, head over her shoulder and smiles. But her eyes stay closed tight even when she gives a try at flinging back her greasy hair breezy like you see on Coke commercials.

What I do is what I have almost never did, which maybe is why my daghter took a wrong turn. But I cannnot stand watching this sad girl act out what she is and I slap her arms away from her hips and push her down into the water, there! She starts up a howling, the shock of water, the shock of my hand which is almost big as hers, and starts trying like she will get back out of our tub, but there is no chance in Creation, because me and my daughter both, dripping wet by now, have got hold of her. And then she does a sensible thing, gives up and lays limp as a rag, which allows us to soap her good, hair too.

As we are working on her I see that her belly has the look like she's going to be a mother, some ways off, only not like my girl/ This one doesn't seem like she's a clue of it, how or even why. And even after sleeping half a day and a night she seems like something that has been pulvriized to brain dead.

I am not the smartest one what ever hit the street. I know this for a fact because if I was then I would have learned in school instead of not, which is what happened in my case. There was in my family a falling apart and fighting and fists flying and childen hiding under their beds hungry and a mama gone too young. It was hillbilly all the way, in the bad sense of hillbillyin. The singing is nice and I can do it still and play the mouth harp too, all that cornball stuff you associate with Arkansas, a state that I got out of fast as lightning, seeing no end in sight to misery and miserbleness rampant in the dust roads and shack houses. What can a chield do? I don't know who in the world expects a child to take care of itself and teach itself right ways and feed itself too if its Caregivers, what the Workers call parents now, if its Caregivers are useless and no good at it. It is a dilemma and causes head scratching and not from lice, either.

Our Roger is getting better, but it's going to take a long time for him to speak right, for him to learn the words, because nobody talked to him for many years and a chiled does not learn right without voices in his ears, speaking soft and kindly words for the joy he wants to be. A childed is always trying to please those it loves and a child in its nature will love everybody . even folks who do it badly, who treat it mean, leave it,. hit it, won't speak to it, won't look in its eyes, say HI.

About this sleepy new girl who come to us like fillings to a magnet, I can't say yet. Roger, though, he may never get right, there is something missing somewhere in him that's more than neglect, but he is been born and is taking up as much space in the world as anybody else. He is to be reckoned with, one way or another, and he will live a long time and be a old man just like ever other not killed in war or shot up with drugs or given the electric chair for bad deeds. To teach a chiled right, to teach a one like Roger, some people ought to get money for doing it.

But what about your own daghter? you are saying. Look at her. Making a baby out of wedlock like any trampy girl, they are a dime a dozen those babies and those dozer girls making them. You got me there. I figure it's genetics, what the teacher at school has been trying to tell us about. The mother makes a baby young, the dagther follows. The mother picks a wrong dad, the daghter don't even try. There's lowlifes that just are, I reckon, and me and mine must be them.

I gaze out the window at the rain sadlly, thinking such about ourselves, me and my daghter and her one Joyann and Roger and this girl we have got with no name, yet, and the only point I can arrive to is, we are here.

III

California

Breakdowns of Any Kind

1970:

There was the time he had that gig in Tahoe, back-up bass for a stand-up comedian-singer, the left-over half of a famous husband and wife team, and Suey, she could talk anybody into anything, followed him there, to the Horseshoe, and was waiting in his room lying spread-legged on the bed and naked except for a suspiciously familiar plaid flannel shirt. "That's Luke's bed! You stole Luke's bed!" was what Daniel exclaimed, the first words he uttered after loud, obscene slurping that she always hated, before he had noticed the shirt, which was, indeed, his dog's bed, hairs and all.

"You're married to that goddamned dog," she said and then he made a big mistake, he knew it was a big mistake even while he was doing it, he crossed the rust-orange rug in his too-tight stage Levis and cowboy boots and made a leap. He intended to land feet first on the bed and pound his chest and make Tarzan noises, another favorite routine of his that she hated. But he had miscalculated, and one leg bumped the night table. He lost his balance and fell between the two double beds, banged his head. The lamp rolled off onto his belly, a heavy thing, turquoise and orange splatters on its fluted base. Then, while he was down and writhing, she had the balls to show him close up her lush, hairy twat, open up the whole works with her long red-painted fingernails. He must have blacked out.

Now he's on the Grapevine, heading back to L.A. after a six-day gig in Reno. It's August and hot as hell even at this late afternoon hour, and the Rabbit, straining up the steep grade, makes chuffing noises. Already losers have pulled off the road, hoods up, fat wives swimming in sweat, leaning against the cars, Bermuda shorts wrinkled in their crotches. The guys under the hoods have slicked-back hair and Adam's apples; their arms are tanned and knotty, their knuckles big. They know how to fix things. If the Rabbit were to overheat and break down, Daniel would have to wait for an emergency vehicle to cruise by; he's not handy, he can't fix plumbing and, for that matter, he can't even manage his old lady. Ever since that time in Tahoe, Suey's been watching him, he can sense her dark-eyed, mean spirit lying in wait just off his right ear, she's psychic when she sets her mind to it. Consequently, his love life on the road is ruined; horny as hell, he hasn't put it to anybody because sure as little green apples she'd lay a curse on him. He imagines crabs, the clap, impotence. When he gets home to the shack on the hillside, he hopes she won't have gone again, taking with her the curtains, chair drapes, throw rugs, bedspread, everything soft. He hopes she'll be sitting in the beanbag chair wide awake, not sleeping much because he hasn't been home, her eyes all red and burnt-looking from staring at an invisible fireplace at night. He figures this fireplace trip of hers is from being raised in Wisconsin. Other than her moods, she's all right. He hopes she'll be zonked but eager and let him lead her to the loft, and that her lips will be soft and her tongue wet.

His dog Luke, an orange shepherd-collie mix who doesn't know how to fetch, is waiting for him, as usual, next to the big eucalyptus, singing in his throat and brush tail wagging, as the car wheezes up the last of the street and pulls into the dirt driveway. The two shacks are still intact, his and the neighbors', Curt and Rosemary; Luke looks fed, and the curtains are still hanging in his windows. What's different is a big tent in the yard where the ping pong table used to be, probably with Curt's mother, who was due to arrive this week, in residence. It was Rosemary's idea, the number with the tent. But something gives with Luke. He doesn't hang around for the unloading of the bass, the guitar, the keyboards. Daniel finds himself talking to himself when he looks behind him.

Inside, the house is tidy and smells of sandalwood incense and cooking. There's Luke, his head in a stranger's lap. His rump is wagging in Daniel's direction but his big brown eyes are on a dark, high-cheeked Mexican-Indian looking dude, a skinny kid, settled comfortably in Daniel's favorite armchair and petting Luke's snout just the way he likes it, lightly caressing the hairs in the wrong direction. "I'm kind of magic with animals. Don't dump on yourself," the kid says. He flicks his long straight hair, held by a beaded sweatband, and looks at the ceiling. "Far-out pad you got here, man. You heard of meteors? They are like wow. You know there is a uptight outa sight witch crashed in a tent on your space? I mean this bitch is the dark mother herself. There's going to be a gig, tonight, on the hill. A happening. Be there or be square. Dig?" He giggles, startling Luke. "Oh, the incipient vocab!"

Daniel, watching this zonked weirdo chuckle to himself, is jealous as hell, because Luke, having stepped back, doesn't turn to his loyal master but waits and moves again into the embrace of a stranger. Then Suey, sounding like somebody from Burbank and wearing no make-up so that Daniel hardly recognizes her, pops up the kitchen stairs. "Hi, honey. How was the show? This is Renan Julio Jesus Ramiriz, a friend of mine. He's an astrologer, a magic kind of guy."

"You can call me Carlos."

Daniel reaches out to shake hands, but Carlos says, "Too cornball, man. I got a image to keep up. Your hair is passe. For gringos, long is gone." Daniel ducks a look into the wall mirror. His hair's parted in the middle and rises up like wings, old-fashioned turn-of-the-century wings on both sides, and drops straight, halfway down his neck. "You want a haircut? I'm real expert with scissors. It's in the blood, man. Heavy Scorpio."

"Suey," Daniel says, thumping down the stairs to the kitchen.

"Can I talk to you?" She's stirring a big pot of what looks like beans and potatoes, her face glistening, hair pulled back into a pony tail. She's wearing the shortest of shorts, cut from an old pair of Levis. A tiny curl of pubic hair escapes one leg. She's the sexiest thing he ever saw. It dawns on him he might be in love, but who is this dude?

At Rosemary and Curt's, connected to Daniel's by a covered walkway, Rosemary is in the kitchen, checking on her roast, the 350-degree oven making the kitchen broil. Curt says his mother Betty is into having meat for dinner, and since it's only her second night with them, Rosemary is going along good-naturedly, because, for one thing, she thinks it's about time she and Curt stopped shacking up and got married. In general she's against meat, because in her personal opinion red meat is bad for arthritis, Adele Davis or one of those food gurus say so. Arthritis is what Betty's shoulders and wrists are suffering from, which is why she's visiting from Minneapolis in the first place: she said she wanted to burn the disease right out of her bones. Although, in Rosemary's opinion, it wouldn't hurt to take a load off them, either.

Rosemary pulls the rubber band out of her long brown hair. She knows she should use those new elastic things, coated with fabric, because she has just shredded a few more hairs and split more ends. She inspects her hair. Just as she thought. She strokes it and puts the rubber band back.

She supposes mashed potatoes are expected, too, and finds a few potatoes to boil. Betty is still in the tent out back and will wait – Rosemary suspects she's into martyrdom – until called to dinner or otherwise invited in. It's clear she isn't going to be underfoot, as Rosemary had feared; but on the other hand, how much peace can a person have, thinking of someone with all those rolls of fat sweating in a tent, while she and Curt are inside with a fan? "Curt?" He's been single-mindedly occupied all afternoon, tidbits of marijuana brownies do wonders to keep his temper down, weaving a special-order shawl for a boutique, and behind schedule, as usual. If she didn't do bagging in a grocery store part time, they'd be, as Daniel says, up shit creek. As it is, the toilet is starting to get sluggish, which is a pain in the duff. "Curt? Do you think your mother is too hot in the tent?" The plumbing in these shacks, theirs and Daniel's, is genuinely disgusting and Mel won't do a thing about it except show up with his plungers and snakes. "Curt? Does your mother like her potatoes medium rare or well done?" Then Rosemary starts giggling and takes the final toke from last night's roach.

What's left of the International Flying Saucer Association, three boys and two girls, sit crosslegged on mats on a large, shaded concrete porch at the top of the hill. The sun is starting to set and the smoggy sky is a vivid, smoky orange. Various members and followers of the group have been living in the big house, on an abandoned estate, for five months, but some of the people got bored and split, a junkie broke all the windows on the north side and had to be tied up and dropped off at Santa Monica beach, two cats died of food poisoning and a girl had a miscarriage on the landing between the second and third floors, which freaked out a number of people. Some thought the mansion was haunted, and two or three others wandered off, taking the last of the communal food money.

The mansion itself is fireproof, even the window sills are metal, designed and etched to look like wood. This was discovered during the rains, when it was cold. Somebody started a bonfire in the entry hall and all that happened was that the marble floor blackened in a few spots and over time evidence of smoke smeared the walls and the door of the elevator that doesn't work because the power is off. The five IFSA members left have been busy painting the upstairs east and west windows in primary colors, using tempera paint they found at an unlocked alternative school down the hill, and they have been sweeping the wide expanse of dirt out front, which they call the landing site, with brooms made when the broom-maker was teaching. Sweeping is an activity they find very satisfying when stoned.

Because the estate has gone back to nature, the outbuildings are overgrown with vines and wild sweetpeas. Until recently, the group has had the run of the grounds, but Lou, a person they suspect of being a militant weirdo, has taken over the potting shed and greenhouse at the south end, along with Moondog, who is howling. "Stupid damn dog," one of the boys says, interrupting his mantra.

Lou, waking from her afternoon sleep, stirs on an Army cot in the gardener's potting shed. Her tiredness is to be expected as the cancer in her breast is healing, and sleep heals, herbs heal, Jesus heals. She has been living in the shed for almost three weeks. She was lucky to find it. It's stone and coolly comfortable, attached to a what must once have been a showcase greenhouse, beds of new life thriving, exotic plants lush with fragrant blossoms. Now the glass is mostly broken, beautiful old pots in shards, the place a general mess. Order, Lou knows, needs to be restored.

So far she has begun decorating her new shelter. Shellacked onto cardboard or scraps of plywood are newspaper clippings and photographs of the war, from *Time* and *The Saturday Evening Post* and *Life*, that hang on the walls or lean against them. She has pictures of the Democratic candidate for governor and Ted Kennedy with an X over his face that she gave him when the jury in April didn't indict him for the death of Mary Jo Kopechne. She has Jack Kennedy saying "Ich bin ein Berliner" and above the head of dear Bobby, slaughtered in the kitchen of the Roosevelt Hotel not far from where she is, she has drawn a halo. She has a large black-and-white double-page spread of Nixon and Kissinger and Spiro Agnew, the sincere one, in the Oval Office. Her collection of Mexican God's-Eyes, made from bright yarn, dangles from the ceiling. As she rises, she makes the sign of the cross.

The dog must sense something is why he's out there busting a gut.

Rosemary sits crosslegged in the kitchen on the wood floor, watching the steam rise from the boiling potatoes. "Curt?" Curt said she had a mean streak a mile wide, which was silly, really, she was just practical. They couldn't have had Betty stay in the house, there wasn't even a proper door on their bedroom, just some wooden beads that she was getting tired of, and there was only one bedroom, besides, and besides that, Betty was staying a whole month, or so the letter on no-nonsense lined school paper in which she invited herself said. As a result of this letter, Rosemary had quite a lot of work to do, moving Daniel's ping pong table and building a deck for the tent and then running wires for electricity so Betty could have a fan, if Curt would get off his duff and find one, as well as light for bedtime reading. She had to borrow the bed, too, and haul it over piece by piece in the VW bus.

She crawls over to the phone and dials, waits and waits because the landlord answers only grudgingly. "Mel? The toilet's plugging again." Maybe it is, maybe it isn't, she can't remember, but the point is, there is a stinky smell and that usually means something's up. Or down. Or rather, not down. Her mind is a riot. She hangs up. "Curt?" She wonders if he's dead over his loom and wonders how her life would change if he were and then the potatoes boil dry and smell terrible and she knows exactly what she'll say at the table. "Think of them as barbequed," she'll say, and they had better eat every last one.

"Would you like dessert?" Suey is asking Daniel, although they never have dessert. "Grape jello with marshmallows." She bats her eyelashes at him. "Yummy."

"You gotta be tolerant," says Carlos. "I have seen it all. This one's a little blown in the brain cells but her heart radiates pure green light. She has got more characters in her than ten normal people. She is rich in this life with all her old personalities trying to find a focus. It makes her psychic. Man, she is one heavy lady. It is, as they used to say in the incipient times, far out."

Daniel thinks of himself as fairly tolerant, but what he wants is for that dog up the hill to shut up, to ball his old lady in peace and then get some sleep. He's too old for the road. He wants to work some quiet, long-term studio gigs. Regular hours, regular work.

"She found me, you see, man, because she was ready. She was up there" – he gestures at the hilltop with a nod – "seeking light, you know, and truth, beauty, stuff like that. A chick gets a certain age, they want that sort of thing, they're tired of messing around –"

His voice goes on but Daniel is amazed by Suey who has turned from the table and is staring off, her long blond hair limp and almost covering her face, tears suddenly dripping down her cheeks. Dripping onto Luke, who doesn't notice, although Daniel can see the dark marks her big tears make in his fur. Daniel doesn't know if he can deal with this. "Wanna joint?" he asks.

Carlos says he isn't into that any more and Suey doesn't seem to hear. Daniel wonders if there's anybody at the club this early, or if he should just go hang out next door. He rolls himself one, licks the paper down.

"She loves you, man," Carlos said. "I seen it in her eyes the first time I made her. She's a real good cook, too."

Daniel looks at Suey, back to Carlos.

"I told you just to test you," he says. "See your reaction, that kind of thing. She can't have kids, you know, that's why she's been up there, to Lou. She wants Lou to cure her. She wants to trap you into marrying her if she can have a baby. But she gave those two she had away, you know, and it's bad karma, she's got to pay. You love her?"

Daniel stands and brushes leaves off his lap. Luke starts licking the floor. Squinting through the smoke, Daniel sucks on the joint a few times before extending it to Carlos. "Oh, well, if you insist. I was raised right, you know, by intellectuals. My mother, however, is in the loony bin just now," and he takes the cigarette and doesn't pass it back.

Suey looks up, eyes streaming, and with a languid hand separates a part through her hair and looks at Daniel. "Just a kid," she says. "Kind of. He never made me, honey, he couldn't get it up. I was going to get back at you for your whoring, but brought him home instead. He was starving up there. I think they were eating dried baboon shit. There's a bunch of weird black pellet-things drying in the sun behind the mansion. Maybe it's prunes, except there's flies all over it. Would flies be so interested in prunes?"

Betty sits on the edge of her bed in the tent, swabbing her perspiring face with a handkerchief. She is dressed for dinner in a navy blue polyester suit with a boxy jacket that she's been told diminishes her bulk; but the practically naked girl her son openly lives with, who wears wrinkled T-shirts she dyes herself and skimpy skirts so short when she bends over you can see her panties, will no doubt think she's overdressed. The tie-dye business with the T-shirt, some Rit and rubber bands as it was described to her, seems like an interesting project for her first graders. Get the mothers to help, at Easter possibly, instead of coloring infernal eggs, you get tired of it year after year, although the children's enthusiasm never wanes, why would it: you forget those little faces are new every fall, because after a while they run together and take on the face of Child Aged Six. They all turn out the same in the end anyway.

It would be lovely to be able to quit, to just plain retire.

But she will not let herself dwell on that one, or the fact of her disastrous visit so far. Curt, like a zombie! And she herself, in a tent! Nor will she whimper because her wrists feel cold, deep inside the bones even though she's suffocating, it must be 100 degrees. The pain, her astrologer said, was probably caused by the transit of Saturn through her sixth house. Afflicted, Saturn can wreak havoc with bones and digestion. Nor will she carry on about the heat rash starting in the folds between breasts and stomach, nor the fact that she ripped one pair of nylons already, on some damn bush.

Starshine, she actually had a youngster last year named Starshine, of all the non-human handles one could give a child. As though he'd simply fallen from the sky. No history there, no sense of those gone before, no family ties.

That damn dog could drive a person batty.

Ting-a-ling. Ting-a-ling. Hasn't the courtesy to come out in person to tell her dinner's ready, not that one. Ring a triangle, like calling ranch hands to chowdown.

"Mother Wiesen, you sit here and Curt, don't go outside just now, I have this thing about slaving all day over a hot stove and people, like, getting to the table while it's still hot and being, you know, appreciative?" Rosemary is plunking down plates, dabbing perspiration from her forehead with the paper napkins she then sets at each place. "You'll have to excuse us, Mother Wiesen, we're not used to, like, sitting down formal? It's a little hairy trying to get it together, while everything's hot. The potatoes are a bit stuck on the bottom of the pan. Curt? So I'll just bring the pan to the table, I don't have serving dishes anyway, who needs them? ha, ha, but anyway, you just make yourself at home, God, it's hot. Curt? Jesus! Excuse me. Back in a sec."

Betty waits, in a chair made from flimsy wood and canvas. If she moves much, she suspects that the canvas seat will split, and down will come baby, cradle and all. She towers over the makeshift dining arrangement, the low round table that she decides used to be a spool for big cable they use to connect the floors of the downtown skyscrapers she can see from the window. The fan at least is pointed her way.

While she waits, she rubs her aching wrists. The smells from the kitchen are heavily garlicky, but at this point she would eat anything. She hasn't seen Curt in almost three years and really did not, did not expect her 4-F son – he thought it was lucky his eyes were so bad! – to be living quite in this manner, although she has heard of hippies. They leave their lives so exposed, they probably don't care if she pokes around. Aside from a strange-looking pipe hidden behind some books – she has some ideas about that! – a half-dozen messy candles, some burnt cones of what she guesses must be incense, the whole house smells vaguely East Indian, she finds on the window ledge a plate of brownies, partly tucked behind a curtain made from the ubiquitous Indian cloth. Curt's still checking on the garden, he always was a nature buff. Rosemary's slammed out after him, they won't miss half of one little piece, she's starving, her system's out of whack, she's still on Eastern time.

Tastes like dirt, the girl isn't much of a cook.

The brownies are probably for the impromptu event later, up on the hill, that the boy staying next door told her about. Bold he was, popped his head right into the tent without so much as a by-your-leave. But not a bad sort, if you just ignored the long hair they all seemed to have and if you weren't afraid of Mexicans or whatever he was. Dark skin is always frightening until you get used to it. This one spoke politely, despite the headband, but she was wary, cool. It's best to keep one's distance.

Now that she thinks about it, he was probably on drugs. His eyes did look strange. Then he came back and told her about something called a "happening" (*Life* or maybe *Time* ran an article on happenings, so she knew what he meant) and he told her about the meteors, which should be lovely.

She's startled when a man entangled in metal augers and carrying a battered tool box and a plunger kicks the screen door. "Hello, excuse me, lady." He uses his foot to pry the door open. "I would doff my hat to meet such a charming lady, if, of course, I was wearing one, but being a worker as I am, I have no such luxuries. Please, not to get up. You wouldn't believe the stories my mother, curses on her to Hades, told me in the old country about the New World, she called it, streets paved in gold, you've read the books about immigrant fantasies, they are a dime a dozen, don't mind my language previous, but some things are not to be forgiven." He shifts his load. "I am the landlord," he continues. "Mel Snow, at your service. The real name you wouldn't believe if you heard it or I could remember it. Please not to mind the interruption. Me, I get no supper, let's not expect too much in this life, a landlord's work is never done. They call, I come. Charmed, I'm sure." He disappears in the direction of the bathroom.

"Here we are," chirps Rosemary, entering through the kitchen door with Curt, sheepish and glaze-eyed, in tow. "The potatoes got burnt, waiting for you to finish communing with nature, but think of it as a barbeque," she says brightly, unfolding the napkin and wiping her brow. "I saw Mel's truck. He come with it? Ha, ha."

The toilet flushes.

In a clearing across from the potting shed, Lou has erected a ten-foot-high cross made of two planks of wood. It was the first thing she did upon finding her new home. On the path in front of the cross, she is busy setting up the card table found on a trash day and rolling into place the tree stumps she uses for stools. Her guests are the two bare-foot men. One has melanomas on the bottoms of his feet, but despite the pain that causes his face to take on a deathly pallor, at twilight he and his friend, both wearing shiny suits slightly baggy at the elbows, climb the hill to join Lou for prayers and supper, a thick soup made with seeds and shoots of plants that grow wild, and her dried horehound tea mixed with manzanita berry cider.

She stirs the pot that hangs over her cooking pit from a sawhorse placed on concrete blocks. As she stirs, she mutters the Lord's prayer, the Catholic version, which seems to her the better bet, being the more popular. She is naked until the barefoot men call out their arrival; healing bodies need to breathe. The doctors have told her the lump in her left breast is definitely cancer, but you can't believe anything that knife-happy crew says. Her son in Vietnam/Cambodia, it's against government policy for his letters to be more specific, is sending herbs that she mixes with the stems of firewood, salsify roots, hemp leaves and plenty of sweet oat grass, all growing in abundance on this abandoned land. While walking through on the morning of her discovering it, she had a vision that the sun was captured in each oat grass kernel; she saw that eating the kernels was partaking of the body of the sun, Nature's version of a communion wafer. She moved from the rooming house in the Valley, where she was biding her time until her son came home. Now Alta Dena dairy delivers raw milk to the top of Aaron Street, where she collects it; and like a natural being, she lives on the milk and the bounty of grasses.

The only difficulty she has encountered in her new life is the heathen young people in the mansion, who are into pillage and defilement. Now they must be setting fire to something, she can smell smoke. Just like them. They tried to paint her cross a watery red, until Moondog scared them off. They ought to be out fighting for their country, doing their God-given duty.

In Daniel's loft Suey turns her head toward the window and inhales. "It's wood smoke, like from I was a kid. Wow. Time warp."

Daniel unwraps his arms from around her hips. Getting her turned on has almost worn him out. "Do you want this or not?" he asks.

"Oh, yes, you are so sexy," she says, robot-like, Daniel thinks. Where did she get that? Probably from *Love Story,* her favorite book. The first time she read it, she mooned around, considering the benefits of contracting a fatal disease. Daniel might then stay by her side. But then, as she said, she thought about the variety of pricks she'd miss and the fact that he'd be getting off on a new chick anyway hardly a week after she bought the farm. Now he starts to tell her to shit or get off the pot, so to speak, but when he raises his head, he smells it too. Smoke.

"Where's Carlos?" she wonders dreamily, like some frigging psychic, he realizes later.

"It's somebody barbequing," says Rosemary. "Don't get uptight about everything, Curt. You're so paranoid."

In the tent, Betty suddenly sits upright and peers through the small mesh window by her side. She is feeling strangely lightheaded and unsettled, and her eyes are dry and won't quite focus. She says aloud to nobody, "It's a fire." It is. A fire. Right there. Very pretty, too, she thinks, the colors at the top of that flame. But there is something she is supposed to be doing. Standing. Shouting. "Fire! Fire!" She hears her voice, which is startling and does get her heart going, but her legs won't move. She is imprisoned in bed. She is going to die trapped in a tent, visiting her only son who is, she realizes suddenly, a stupid ass.

Mel hears the flames from the bathroom where he's taking a crap, trying out the flushing business, and listening to Curt complain to Rosemary about the smoky smell. He himself can't smell his way out of a paper bag, but his ears, his ears should be on one of those detective dogs, he hears the crackling like when you crumple papers, such a waste, before throwing them into the incinerator. God in hell, when he stands up he can't believe it, in the almost-dark he sees grass on fire and a tent in its way, too close to the house, both houses, his whole investment in this fucking new world, gone, ashes to ashes like life itself, and him with no insurance, who would insure such fire hazards?

As the evening star rises, the fire is licking the tent, beginning to sear through the canvas. One of its anchoring ropes has snapped, and the tent is askew. Curt, glasses slipping down his nose, emerges from the house on the run with a pitcher of water, Rosemary squealing behind. He tosses and misses, splatting the patio stones. Removing his shirt, he slaps at the flames as he's seen in the movies, when he hears his mother coughing from inside the tent, holy shit. He turns to see Rosemary trying to unsnarl the hose, just as Daniel tosses him one end of a blanket. They start flapping. Suey stands in the doorway of Daniel's in her baby dolls, bare-assed, counting heads. She steps into the bloomers she's been carrying, then saunters toward the tent. Rosemary has the hose untangled but the water only trickles. Mel, struggling up a ladder he's dragged from the back of his truck in order to wet down the roof, is hollering for the hose. Betty emerges from the tent on Suey's arm. "She's stoned out of her gourd," Suey says to nobody in particular. "She was my mother in another life, and Carlos must have knew I owed her. Far out."

The hose reaches only to the steps leading up to patio. Rosemary organizes Daniel and herself into a pitcher brigade. Suey is crooning over Mother Wiesen and Curt is cursing and following them from the hose to the tent and back again. "Where is that bastard? I know who did this. That freak, that freak you're harboring, Daniel. Some refugee from the funny farm. No! Some undercover Yippie asshole …"

The tent is soaked but saved. While Curt falls silent, glaring into space, Daniel and Rosemary walk around him, winding hose. Rosemary's thinking that the bedding will have to be changed. She wonders if they have enough sheets.

"Such language," says Betty to Curt. Suey thinks she's having a delayed reaction. She sits her down on a bench under the lemon tree, where they're surrounded by trampled geraniums. Betty smiles at Suey. "I think my arm is bruised from where I silly fell out of bed. I think it's broken. I think maybe it's burned."

Curt perks up, hearing what his mother says. He locates a piece of two-by-four left over from the construction of the tent platform. Muttering "Frigging bastard!" he starts up the hill.

Mel is putting the ladder away when he sees Curt heading up, slashing at weeds in his path. "Judas priest, we must grab him! Crazy man! Who knows what questions the pigs will come with if he kills the son of a bitch?"

There is a moment of silence.

"Mel's a Communist," Suey tells Betty.

"Jesus," Daniel says, looking toward his exposed patch of thriving homegrown. Curt has pushed through the hedge and is out of sight. They can hear him crashing through the tall grass, twigs snapping. "This will be fun, Mother, swear to God," says Suey, taking Betty's elbow. "Lou can heal you, she's a white witch. That's the good kind. It's real darn pretty up there. Do you know the meteors are happening? Up in the sky? It will just blow your mind, really and truly. Do you know what meteors are? Are you scared of dogs, Mother?"

They are shadows, savages keeping beyond range of the white man's camp and the white man's nasal voices. Their faces painted blue, with yellow dabs above their brows, they creep around the edges of the trespasser's claimed territory. The poster paint is drying and their faces are beginning to crack and itch. They are stoned and curious about the fire down the hill. The barefoot men whom they recognize from other evenings are perched on the stumps, side by side, eating soup, surrounded by tall grass, backs against a tree on the crest of the hill. The tree is a stubby California oak with many twisted branches. It has grown tilted into the wind, bending toward the sea in the distance that glistens darkly around the hulls of lighted ships in the harbor at San Pedro. The girls knew someone from there once. Overhead a DC10 from LAX leaves a trail moving east. In the deepening twilight, two lights are noticed in the sky. The twinkling evening star and Mars, red and unblinking, the violent star, according to some astrologer who once passed through; if you have Martian energy you are angry all the time and like to set fires. Carlos is into that sort of thing. They've seen his chart.

Moondog is tracking shadows. Curt is thrashing around nearby, yelling and cursing, lost in some prickly overgrowth. Carlos, who has been hiding in the greenhouse chewing his fingers and talking to himself, makes a break for it. He approaches the group, head bowed and murmuring benedictions.

Lou and Rosemary organize a healing circle, everyone linking hands, except for Curt, who refuses to join, and Betty. She's lying on a mat some distance away, snoring. Mel doesn't mind the circle business, he's next to Suey whom he's always suspected of having the hots for him. Her hand is cool but moist. Curt says, "I can't believe you people. I fucking can't believe it. He was trying to kill my mother."

"He takes too many drugs," Rosemary whispers to one of the barefoot men beside her. "It gives him a one-track mind, you know?"

"Your mother is a capitalist," says Carlos, his voice reasonable.

"She's a school teacher, for Christ's sake."

"Don't take the Lord's name in vain," admonishes Lou. "Picture white light. Picture perfection in all things."

"She works for the state, she's against the brown and black classes rising up for freedom," says Carlos. "You people need radicalizing something desperate."

Suey lets go of Mel's hand and wanders off to the wild garden under Lou's cross.

"That's a crock! Where are you at, man? She's a harmless old lady, doing a job, for Christ's sake."

"Has anybody seen a meteor yet? I did," says Suey. "Just now."

"Who the fuck cares, when this peabrain practically set the world on fire?"

"Don't make waves, old buddy," says Daniel, shaking out his hands. "What's done is done."

"Don't exaggerate, Curt," says Rosemary. "It wasn't the whole world, really, it was only a five-by-five patch of dirt, approximately, in our yard."

"It was our space, you got that? Our space and this loony –"

"Your space, my eyes," says Mel, letting go of Rosemary. "It's my property, my livelihood, my only income. That screwy kid –"

"Forgive me," Carlos says, moving towards Lou and the barefoot men. "I've, like, been homeless too long, you know? Like I kinda lost it there for a second, I guess I was remembering my old teacher. What grade she teach?" he asks Curt.

"First."

"Right. Remembering my old first grade teach and how she hated me, man, just hated me. I always had to sit in the corner. That's why I did it. Kind of a long-term revenge strategy."

"He needs to go to Nam, swear to God," Suey says, eating nasturtiums. "He's got the mentality. He's hooked on blood and guts. It's where he's at."

"I'm, like, into flowers, myself," says Rosemary.

"A lightweight," pipes up the other barefoot man. "What this country needs is stiffer backbones. Heroes and brave men. Down with ban-the-bombers."

"Curt's feet are bleeding," Suey says, chewing. "You know?"

"He tried to kill my mother."

"Are you guys fruits?" Mel asks the two barefoot men.

"What's done is done, man," says Daniel, yawning.

"I wish we had some marshmallows and a fire," says Rosemary. "Marshmallows would be, you know, far out."

"No fucking fires," says Curt.

There is silence, except for Moondog, who is growling from somewhere.

Carlos spreads his arms. "People of the planet. Close your eyes and see in your mind's eye the vaulted heavens. Visualize the eternal pyramid."

"I'm sick of all this visualizing shit," Suey says, wandering back. "I want to have a store. Like sell things. Little bottles and colored ribbons, shit like that."

"We're all there is in the universe," says Lou. "Would anybody like tea? We're God's chosen lambs, each one."

"I think God would have better taste," Suey says. "I mean, like, the trees are all right, but the clothes stink." She spits out a wad of stems. "Rosemary's pregnant and doesn't even know it."

"Balls. If we're all there is, God is dead. You're talking accident here, a serious accident." It's a voice from the dark. Moondog begins to bark excitedly.

"I'm pregnant?"

"It's going to grow up and have purple hair. Or maybe it'll be bald. It'll call you names. It'll be mean."

Betty rubs her eyes. She has heard voices and then growling in her ear, she has felt something sniffing her feet. It's dark, except for a smattering of stars. She sees a meteor shoot past, and then that nice boy who visited her in the tent is looking down at her. "Oh, hello," she says. And when he doesn't reply, she tries to speak his language. "Where's the happening?"

"You're it," says Carlos and she hears giggling, but she doesn't know what they mean by it, or who they are.

The Next Governor
of California

Jude is perched upright on the daybed, stoned and working on controlling her lips. In her living room are two cops, a younger, Mexican one and an older blond one. They look like clowns to her, wearing their phony somber faces. For one thing, they're trying to get Jason. She can see it in their eyes, that bureaucratic hunger for what they think is an orphaned five-year-old. The cops don't like her, she can tell by the way they won't touch anything, even the arms of the wobbly director's chairs they're facing her in, as though the arms would be dirty and should be scrubbed with Brillo. If they don't like her, they certainly wouldn't like her cousin Rita, who doesn't even believe in germs.

"It's been two weeks and a couple of days since the boyfriend reported her missing," says the blond, leaning towards Jude, indicating the suitcase and some boxes abandoned in the corner. They're talking about Rita, who left some things behind and hasn't bothered to let Jude know where she is. "Tell us about this guy. Besides the incident with the gun when he threatened you."

With Rita's kid Jason down the hill visiting his babysitter, out of her hair for awhile, Jude had managed to do a load of laundry and throw on some clean bellbottoms and her favorite earrings, battered bronze, like warrior shields for ears. In peace and quiet, she read part of a chapter in the sociology text she was supposed to study for her summer school class at Cal State. She rolled a joint and toked it twice, then had to snub it when she saw the same two cops who had been over before come wading through the weeds, past Daniel's place, on toward hers.

Jude uses both palms to wipe perspiration off her face. "He didn't really threaten us." She has told the story before. Rick said he wanted to see Rita. The gun was his way of getting Rita's attention, because she had broken up with him. Rita called him a jealous maniac, but Jude thought any guy could get that way. Rita had sort of a reputation for fooling around.

When Jude looks up, Jason is back, eating a cherry popsicle that's dripping stickiness all over the backs of his hands. "Is Rick crazy, Auntie Jude?" Jude thinks about Rick's tiny, wet eyes behind blind-man-thick glasses. He could've shot her through the heart, by mistake. She tries to focus again on the questions the cops are asking, about Rita's plan to go up north to work on a political campaign. Jason is squirming in the beanbag chair, and the gristly rustle is getting on her nerves. Murmuring to each other, the cops start in about the Santa Cruz murders. The Mexican must think she has tuned out. He raises his voice to ask her, "Santa Cruz is on the way to where your cousin was headed, isn't that right?"

Jude slides a glance at Jason. His lips are so pressed together they have disappeared into his mouth. "Hey, there's a kid here," she says mildly. The cops give each other a look. They've been doing that all along, staring at her, then dropping their eyes, sneaking peeks at her boobs. She's not wearing a bra under her T-shirt.

"You girls should be more careful," the blond one says, changing the subject, sounding like Uncle Henry, Rita's dad. Rita would have a fit at how Jude is passively smiling at these chauvinists. Jude and Rita are practicing consciousness-raising and trying to think of themselves as women instead of "gals" or "girls" or "young ladies". But Jude isn't giving the pig hell for saying "girls" because she doesn't want to get busted. Rita, on the other hand, wouldn't give a damn.

The cop shifts. The chair squeaks with his weight. "What about the boy?"

Jason springs out of the nest he's made in the beanbag and plunks himself in the wooden rocker that Jude's ex-boyfriend painted blood red just before she went and had the abortion anyway. He rocks fast, holding the cleanly licked popsicle stick neatly between two fingers. He has Rita's round grey eyes and they're fixed on Jude. "His dad's coming to get him while Rita's away. Next week," she says, making a face. Jude doesn't like Rita's ex. He's dumb and slicks his hair back with grease. Jason takes after Rita's side.

The cop stands and clears his throat. The other one follows suit. "Keep praying, Miss, don't give up hope. For the boy's sake." Jude squints up at him. She thinks there must be a cop school somewhere that teaches them all to sound like Iowa. The Mexican ducks through the curtain of faded wooden beads that separates the living room from the kitchen. He tips his hat at her and pulls open the kitchen door. "You should get locks," he says. She has been thinking about it. She went to a hardware store and looked at some.

The big jade plant growing beside the porch looks dry. When she remembers to, Jude throws dish water on it to save the drains. She leans against the door frame and watches the cops pick their way down the overgrown path. "I told her not to go that night," she says. "With Rick. I told her." But they have rounded Daniel's house and are out of range. A cricket snaps in the grass where they've been. Jude rubs her upper arms to get warm. She always feels cold when she smokes dope. It's getting dark, but still the breeze is hot. Another scorcher tomorrow.

"How come you told a fib, Auntie Jude?" Jason tugs at her T-shirt. She looks at him and he pulls his hand back as though she would bite him. She wants to holler at Rita, wring her damn neck. This kid is hanging on her when she should be getting it together to study. And the clowns keep showing up, eyeing her. "Go wash your hands," she says.

She supposes that once again she has to find them something to eat. She could be happy nibbling a bread crust with a hunk of butter on it or a few tablespoons of corned beef hash cold from the can, but a kid seems to need more. Rita is very organized. Her cupboards are full of cream soups, cream of mushroom and tomato and celery, and from these, along with some spices, a few vegetables and a piece of meat, she can make anything. After a day with her class of first graders, Rita sails into the apartment on Pico, above the Mexican restaurant, drops her books and purse and twenty minutes later the place smells as though a full-time mother is at home. Studying in Rita's living room, she has heard their voices, Jason's and Rita's, his reciting what happened in kindergarten, or at Day Care. She has heard them laughing together, because Rita is energetic and patient and always did know how to listen if she knew you needed it.

Then Rita became political. Watergate made her decide to stand up and be counted, she told Jude earlier in the summer, over a bottle of Chianti and with the spatting and sputtering of some candle stubs Jude managed to find for the table. Rita had decided to take a semester off from teaching, to work for what she believed in. That's why she was going to northern California to help on the campaign for the guy she called the next governor. Jude should have wrung her neck when she had the chance. "Mommy believes in the future," Jason had piped up more than once in Rita's absence. Just the sort of idealistic bullshit that Rita would tell the kid while planning to dump him on his dad for three months.

Jude bites her fingers and thinks, Phone, damn it. She closes the door and pushes aside the cafe curtains and rests her forehead against the warm glass. The little ruffly curtains smell dusty. Rita sewed them herself and they look like it, weird hems and peculiar bunches. They were a housewarming present for Jude's first place.

Jason has come up behind her and is tapping his foot. He says, "Maybe we better go to my house and unplug the fish tank?"

Jude turns slowly and stares at him. She feels her mouth might be hanging open. He stands blinking at her, as though he has something in his eye. He's wearing one of Rita's stances, a hip flung forward, legs rooted, chin high. Just three days ago when they went over to the apartment, he wouldn't let her unplug the damn tank. They were aerating it, he insisted. When his mommy came back they were going to buy three albino tiger barbs and three red oscars.

"Make up your mind," Jude shrugs, reaching out to yank the tail of his belt, pulling him off balance. The belt is too long, a Gene Autry with lots of fake silver. She tucks the end through the loops in his jeans. "Did you feed Golda like I told you?" One thing she's learning, you have to keep on a kid all the time. Golda Meir is mostly Rita's rabbit that she lets Jason take care of. Jude is not a fan of rabbits except in stews, and Jason knows it. He's off like a shot.

At the kitchen table, eating corned beef hash with melted cheese on it, Jude suddenly feels gouged in the lower belly. She thinks of the pain as dues pain. She screwed carelessly and got pregnant, but she's not Rita, she couldn't deal with a kid. The pain is starting to come in mid-month and doubles her over, as though the ovaries were on strike, she told Rita, refusing to part with their eggs after she did what she did. Her biology was pre-women's-lib.

"Can you smell the yukky?" Jason asks. He's trying to make conversation again. But he's right, Jude does get a whiff of the sweet rot from the boiled fox skull. The stink wafts out unexpectedly from secret places, though she has scrubbed the stove and the floor with Lysol and sprays lilac all around once in a while, which she realizes might not be a great idea. The mix can leap out at you unexpectedly and make you want to barf.

"Yeah." She wrinkles her nose. "Great find," she says, reminding him of the afternoon they were up on the hill, Rita packed and the two of them staying at Jude's for a week or so to get away from Rick, who had started hanging around. They climbed the trail to the abandoned estate, to watch the sunset. Then while Jude was sitting on a boulder, smoking, Jason came whooping up, slapping his thighs and being Hi-ho Silver. He stopped in his tracks and shouted. "Bones! Dead bones! A whole face!" Jude jumped to her feet, shrieking, and Rita laughed. In the grass near where Jude had been sitting, Jason had spotted a fox skull, small and almost delicate when looked at up close. Its snout was broken at the very tip and a fly was cleaning itself in the cavity. Of course Jason wanted it for Show and Tell, and of course it had been Jude who ended up carrying it down, under the fence, past the pepper tree, back to the house. Because you're bravest, Rita had said teasingly, flipping her gypsy skirt and keeping a straight face.

Jude looks at Jason, who is politely pushing his fork around in the pile of tiny square-cut potatoes, congealing in grease, with lumps of unmelted cheese on top. He hates corned beef hash, but he hasn't eaten even the cheese. It's Velveeta, and he likes that. "It's not your fault," she says.

After they found the skull, Jude had gone straight to crash on the daybed in front of the T.V. and Rita and Jason went into the kitchen to do the boiling business. Rita swore on a stack of Bibles that a little vinegar in water and two hours' boiling would make the skull clean as a whistle.

Jason's watching her every move as she lights another cigarette. He has started following her around like a shadow. "Hey," she says. "You could go watch T.V." But he shakes his head. Ever since Rick and the gun, he won't even watch "Gunsmoke". "Look for something funny. There must be something funny on. Go on." He pushes his chair back from the table and puts his plate in the sink, as Rita has trained him. "Thanks, Auntie Jude," he says, a habit she'd like to break him of. He thanks her for some crud he didn't even eat.

She swallows an Excedrin and takes her cigarette outside and sits on the steps. The moon isn't up yet. It will rise through the branches of the eucalyptus trees scattered along the crest of the hill, beyond Daniel's side of the yard. Her eyes are tired, but she wouldn't sleep, she knows. Since Rita left, she has lain awake or else dozed fitfully, listening for a rustle in the grass that might be someone sneaking up on them. She listens for Rick's return, or Rita playing a joke. She listens for Rita's giggle under her window.

She sniffs the fragrance of the lemon tree in the warm air. "Bewitched" is on T.V. That afternoon while Rita and Jason were in the kitchen boiling the skull, she must have dozed off, because she remembers all of a sudden Rita appeared, rasping in her ear. Jason was

patting her face with a cold, sweaty hand. She thought there was an
earthquake or that she was sick, maybe dying and didn't know it, they
were both taut like rubber bands before you zing them.

"Somebody's out there."

"So who is it?" The T.V. was off. It could have been morning for all
she knew.

"A nut of some kind," breathed Rita.

"We think it's a man with a gun, Auntie Jude," Jason said, which
made Jude sit up. The kid, for all he could bug her, wasn't easily fooled.

She tiptoed to the back door, a half-door-half-screen thing, and
peered out. In the twilight was the figure of a balding guy, maybe wearing glasses, under one of the lemon trees. In the light from Daniel's
bathroom window, it looked like something was gleaming in his hand.
She stared at the palm tree that rose above Daniel's house and imagined the three of them, Jason and Rita and her, trucking down the
stairs and going about their business, digging around in the cupboards
for something to eat. Rita maybe putting together one of her specials.

But a horrible smell was making her queasy. The vinegar gave it
away. She turned and shook a finger at Jason and Rita, who had crept
up behind her. "Do you mean to tell me you have got that skull down
there, boiling like mad? Do you smell that?" She sounded just like her
mother, voice high-pitched and clipped, no-reprieve. Rita peeked
through the screen and gasped. In retrospect Jude realizes that Rita's
gasp should have been a clue that out there was somebody she knew,
but at the time Rita didn't say anything. Instead, Jason said something
pathetic, like "Mommy?" in that quavery voice he sometimes got that
Jude couldn't stand.

"I don't intend to harm anyone," the nut said. Rita started whim-
pering then.

As soon as he spoke, Jude saw the gun in his left hand. "Everything's going to be fine," she shushed the two behind her, wishing she
were stoned because then her nerves would calm down. "Just stay out
of my hair. And sit. Jason." Jason sat, Indian-style like they made him
do in kindergarten, and Rita hunkered down.

It was Rita's movement of "hunkering down", as Jude saw it, that reminded her of line of fire that you heard about on the T.V. news, when they were talking about hijackings and hostage-takings. The way the bullet would go. What she saw was that it would enter her in the bony place at the base of the throat and blow out the big neck bone at the top of her spine and smash Jason's crayoned tropical fish picture that Rita had framed with one of those black frames from Woolworth's. The bullet would shatter the glass, which would fall in pieces all over his sleeping bag; and then it would nestle in the painted wood wall, or go on through.

The tip of the gun slapped a shoulder-high branch, the sound making Jude jump out of her skin, and a lemon, small and hard, plopped on the ivy-covered ground. She saw the creep's feet planted in shoes with tassles. Behind his back her neighbor Daniel's face popped into the frame of his lit bathroom window.

"Don't get me wrong," the creep said. "I just want to talk. To Rita."

Rita was cowering behind her hands, when Jude looked, with tears streaming down her cheeks. "Oh God, if he finds out, he'll kill me," Rita whispered, a sure sign the creep was her boyfriend Rick and that she had been messing around. Jude's heart was still hammering. She wanted to slap Rita good. Kick her right down the stairs.

"Get out," she said.

Then she spotted Daniel in his new shirt, a neon-bright Hawaiian print from K-Mart, tiptoeing barefoot across his patio, past his homemade ping-pong table. "I'm gonna call the cops," she said, loud. Rita groaned, "He wouldn't hurt a fly. Don't hurt him, don't hurt him." As though Jude could or Daniel were a Green Beret and not a part-time musician at the Valley Holiday Inn. Daniel spoke up from behind the oleander. "Hey, buddy, are you sure this is what you want?"

"It has real bullets in it," Rick cried, swinging the gun.

"Rick, oh Rick," crooned Rita.

Jude remembers having been frightened all along, yet still, somehow, living behind glass, safe in T.V.-viewer land. When Rick told them the gun was loaded, her knees started shaking, she felt lightheaded. "It has real bullets?"

"Yeah," he said, swiveling back.

"You want to spend the rest of your life in jail? Are you bonkers?" The pistol wavered. "No. I want to see Rita. I love her." His lips were thick and petulant. He would kiss like dog slobber. Rita must be crazy.

"Rick, oh Rick," moaned Rita.

"Yeah, buddy," Daniel said. "But she's afraid of you, you know?"

"Afraid of me?" As though it were new notion. Go ahead, Jude remembers thinking, ask why. Then the creep had an idea. You could tell because his eyes behind the glasses blinked fast. "You're fooling around with her."

Their voices lobbed back and forth like ping pong balls. Jude was trapped and starving, she was tired and feverish, and she was smelling rotten fox bones boiling dry in her kitchen. "PUT DOWN THAT GODDAMN GUN," she bellowed. "DROP IT!"

He did and Daniel jumped him and then in slow motion they both keeled over into the ivy.

Rita leapt up and skittered down the steps. Daniel rolled off Rick and grabbed the gun. Carried it with both hands to Jason and Jude. "Motherfucker's really loaded," he said, whistling through his teeth.

Jude lights another cigarette. Then, the way it went, Loverboy, back on his feet, started bawling Rita out. Jason touched the gun, ran a finger along its shiny barrel, before either Jude or Daniel, his hands still trembling, noticed, because they were both watching Rick and Rita under the lemon tree. They watched from the doorway as Rick slapped Rita's bottom, poked her and squeezed her. Jude waited for Rita to knock his block off. She waited for Rita to flounce back upstairs. Instead, Rita stood leaning into him, taking it. At one point she wiggled free and looked up at them, trying to catch Jude's eye.

"Go on," said Jude, angry and sick to her stomach. "You said he wouldn't hurt a fly."

Rita winked and blew a kiss at Jason, who had joined them on the porch. Rick took Rita's hand and the two of them disappeared around the thicket of bougainvillea at the corner of Daniel's house. Daniel put his arm around Jude's shoulders. Jude remembers fighting back tears.

She remembers thinking she intended to tear that bitch apart the next morning. Piece by piece.

Daniel went home and Jude and Jason turned off the burner in the kitchen. The smell of boiled bones made them gag. Using old dishtowels and scarred potholders, they carried Jude's pot down the driveway in the moonlight, walking sideways like crabs. Jude was so much taller than Jason, that even though they were careful, the bit of hot stinky slop left in the pot splashed out on his side. They heaved the pot into the garbage can, and Jude pressed the lid on as tightly as it would go.

Afterwards, she put Jason to bed with his teddy bear and paced in the living room. She didn't toke up, because she thought she ought to be alert, like a guard. After a while, she opened a window and listened. On the porch, Golda Meir scratched in her cage. She closed the window and blew her nose again on the roll of toilet paper she was carrying around with her, but the smell of the bones stayed in her nostrils.

She thought about the smell that burning bodies have, but she hadn't known what it was, the time as a kid hanging on the schoolyard fence, fingers curled through the holes. Firemen across the street, the siren pulling the children from Tag and Rover Come Over and the upside down-hanging bars, which is where Rita had been, showing her panties and na-naing at a group of tittering girls. That had been Rita in fourth grade. She wouldn't give up being a tomboy even though Auntie Alice always had her girls wear dresses. Jude couldn't remember what she herself might have thought of doing if she hadn't been as usual watching Rita from the primary yard. Then the fire trucks and the playground tilting to the back fence and the little wood house with the junky yard burning brightly, flaming, and black smoke and firemen pulling spraying hoses and teachers shooing and scooting.

She toes out her cigarette, the back of her throat hot and dry. She's smoking too much. At Daniel's a door bangs. He saunters into the yard, singing to himself, probably stoned, and snaps on the spotlight over the ping pong table. Through the screen she hears Jason tossing on his cot. She remembers hearing him tossing all night after Rita left.

Daniel begins playing ping pong with his dog Luke, trying to teach Luke to fetch but Luke doesn't get it, wags his tail and drools. He's part border collie and part something else, eyes dense brown globes in orange fur. Jude hears the ping, "Damn," pong, "Come on, Luke, jeez Luke" and the sound of Daniel scrabbling in the bushes for the ball while Luke watches and drools and wags. The moon, a sliver of a crescent, finally rises.

Daniel is fed up with Luke and gives him a lecture. "Listen here," he says, "you listen here." And Luke does, he's all ears.

They begin phoning. Rita's mom and dad, Jude's Auntie Alice and Uncle Henry, calling from Nebraska, wanting to see their baby. It was a primary instinct, Auntie Alice says, that caused her to wake bolt upright one morning and think, Some one of us is missing. At first Jude thinks they mean Jason when they talk about wanting to see their baby, but they mean Rita, the last of five. They are sending money by registered mail, and any time Jude thinks best, they'll fly out to have a little talk with that young man, that candidate person, they'll get to the bottom of what's what, and is Judy sure Rita hasn't been kidnapped by that bunch, the Children of God?

Cousin Harold. Cousin Sue. Regina talking about her brood, forgetting for a minute why she called. Her own mom, senile before her time, but with memories that come out of the blue and zap you. "You were always careless," says Jude's own mom, for no reason but for plenty. In the midst of the family calls, Rita's ex phones. He has business in Yuma, so he'll pick up Jason late. He calls him "the boy". "I'll pick the boy up a few days late," he says. He names a day, and Jude hollers it out to Jason. Then one of the campaign managers for the next governor phones, wondering where the text for the convention flyer is. Soon, Jude has a cheery spiel down pat. She says that Rita just got carried away, side-tracked, you know how involved she gets when she's into something. "But have you heard from her?" Uncle Henry wants to know, again.

Now two weeks and six days since the incident with the gun, as the cops called it, she still hasn't heard from Rita. The heat of summer could kill you. The pain in her belly is getting worse. Jude thinks her uterus is infected.

"Jude," Jason says, tugging at her jeans in that pesky way. "Jude." She's on antibiotics and feeling spaced out, smoking and washing dishes, the cigarette becoming soggy on the edge of the counter where it's propped. "Hey, Auntie Jude," Jason says. "It smells smoky outside." She is thinking. She doesn't know how to deal with Rita's apartment. The rent's overdue and Rita hasn't left her any signed checks. She wonders if she should use Uncle Henry's money.

"Smoke, Jude!"

"Will you be quiet?" To placate the kid, she dries her hands on a dish towel and steps outside. She looks up. The hill is on fire. Up behind the greasewood that separates the house from the acres of unoccupied land above, flames are crackling. Just yards from the pepper tree.

Jude stares. She turns and shakes Jason. "Get in the car." The siren she has been hearing without paying attention is suddenly loud, and close. The fire engine, rumbling and gearing down, labors up the street from the boulevard below. She and Jason get as far as the driveway when the firemen arrive, dragging hose and cursing. She can hear the fire sizzling, followed by windy-sounding roars.

Jason starts yelling. "Golda! Golda!"

Jude grips his arm and watches the firemen tromp through Daniel's yard, past the one row of sorry corn supposed to shield the thriving homegrown. Daniel is out of town, on a three-day gig. She wonders if she can get arrested.

"Take that kid!" one of the firemen barks at her.

"My teddy! Tesha-bear! Luke! Golda!" Jason is screaming, jumping like a pogostick. "Golda! Golda!"

"Get in the car!"

But Jude can't back out because the fire truck is parked behind her. They sit in the car, Jason shivering, teeth ground tight, the skin of his jaw pulled down like somebody having a spasm. Jude stares at his face, then drags him out her side and starts down the hill with him in tow. Luke, who has been hiding under the car, slips out and follows them. Neighbors and strangers are gathered at the top of the street. Someone says he spotted the fire from the freeway and called the fire department from a Shell station. Eleven-year-old Lupita, Jason's babysitter, finds him and opens her arms. Jude looks at the girl's chunky body, already soft, that Jason hides in. Lupita's mother, who sells tamales that she makes from her kitchen, gestures to Jude about going back for clothes. Jude doesn't care about clothes, she's listening to the kid blubbering to Lupita about the damn rabbit. She's watching ashes drift by and thinking about the T.V. news from the night before, more on the Santa Cruz murders. They have found body parts, ravaged as though by wolves. They have found chewed bits.

Jude strokes back up the hill through the smoke, swimming through the dead heat. She sees the cage with a dark shape heaped at the bottom. For a moment she lets herself think it's a creature just taking a snooze. Kid's bunny dies of smoke inhalation, the news might say. Jude slaps her hand over her bawling mouth. She can't save a fucking thing.

Daniel's yard is trampled and soaking, the ping pong table upended, one leg snapped; the garden a muddy patch. Looking from Daniel's place to hers, she wouldn't know anything unusual had happened. Her daisies and the lemon trees are untouched.

Jude takes Jason's hand and leads him to Golda Meir's cage. "Oh, no!" she exclaims. "I must have left the cage open by mistake this morning. Jeez, Golda's escaped!" She just bets the rabbit took off like a shot when the fire started. She just bets. And now Golda is gone, free at last.

His eyes fill, but Jude figures he understands freedom. "You want to hunt for her?"

He shakes his head no. "Mommy forgot to say goodbye too."

After Jason is in bed, Jude sits outside on the steps. The air smells of smoke. She thinks that maybe they didn't, Cheryle Sue and her ugly brother that everyone hated, actually burn up. Maybe it was smoke inhalation, the two of them in the upper bunk holding on to each other, instead of eating at the cafeteria like lucky boys and girls. Rita said that Cheryle Sue and her brother were going to play hookey because of the piano lessons in the auditorium after lunch. Because the week before, Cheryle Sue couldn't remember the dozen notes they all had to play, their hands holding invisible palmed balls over the keys and placing them, not plunk or thunk but lightly and gracefully, the teacher said, lightly and gracefully as landing doves, wrists loose and elbows flexed, plunk, plunk, plunk, plunk – plunk, went Cheryle Sue. Who had a freckled face and carroty hair, thick black eyebrows and eyes too close together. That's what Rita said. Cheryle Sue had to play it again but she couldn't, Rita said, couldn't do anything but stand, head down and ashamed. The teacher said Cheryle Sue had to try harder and practice at home, but of course everybody knew Freck-leface didn't have a piano at home or to borrow at church either, because they probably didn't even go to church, their mother was divorced.

Later, crosslegged on the living room carpet, Jude throws the I Ching coins. The hexagram speaks of clouds and thunder, difficulty at the beginning, furthering through perseverance. It apparently would further her to appoint helpers, but she can't think of any.

The next afternoon, when Jude returns from the grocery store, Jason is on the porch, his suitcase packed, Golda's empty cage beside him, and on his lap, his pillow with the bright yellow-gold case that Rita made. "What are you doing?" Jude wants to know.

"Dad's coming today, Auntie Jude. Don't you remember?"

By dark, she convinces him to come inside. She's made brownies, two batches. One for him and one for her.

After traveling all morning, Jason finally has given up snuffling and is lying like a zombie against the door in the front seat. His dad won't be able to find him, he has said, if they're driving somewhere, but Jude thinks this is a good reason, all by itself, for going. During the night, she remembered how she always sensed in Rita's ex a killer mentality. She thinks maybe it wasn't Rick, after all.

As for Rick, the cops have nothing against him, no proof; he comes to the station almost every day to check on any findings and he cries and says he loves her. All his guns are registered.

It's going to be one of those unsolved cases Southern Cal is full of. This is what the Mexican cop told her on the Q.T. Rita could have been shot by the boyfriend, temporarily deranged, a dude who would never kill again. Happen anywhere. Some beach we haven't checked yet. Inna desert. She ain't coming back except if she can on her own steam, in her own time. Female bodies: they find them roasting on hillsides at the end of summer.

The window's down, Jude's hair is blowing free, snapping her cheeks and throat. She has tried to humor Jason, tried to be fun. Partly to stay awake, she started a game of counting telephone poles, but he wasn't having any of it. She got to 56 on her side before she quit. She's hot enough to melt and they haven't anything to drink. In the rearview mirror she glimpses her face, the hollows in her cheeks pronounced, the circles under her eyes.

She left a note for Rita that had their lives in it and that over the night of working on it shrank to When they left and Why they left, and p.s. they'd phone.

"Welfare's coming for me, Jude," Jason had said. When he said it, it was past his bed time and he had brownie crumbs stuck in the corners of his mouth. His sprinkling of freckles stood out on his pale face. It's true, they had phoned. Child Welfare wanting to know things. Closing in on him. How old was Jude? Was she married? For Jude, it was the bureaucrats figuring Rita was dead, when really, Rita was just off on a lark.

When the candidate himself phoned, he agreed. Right away he said, She's off on a lark, you know how she is, and Yes yes yes that's exactly what Jude thought. Everything will be all right, he went on to say, it always is in the long run. Jude came down, slapped in the face with a wet hanky. "Yeah, yeah," she said, but eventually hung up in a fog of failing hope. She wanted to get laid. She wanted a baby. She wanted dead creatures to breathe again. She wanted the flesh of the fox between her teeth. She wanted the fox flashing through woods and safely out of her sight, his stink out of her nose.

Jason scrambles to his knees and lets out a shout, "Smoke, Jude!"

She looks into the back seat. The fiery tip of her cigarette is embedded in his pillow. The pillow is smoking.

She signals and pulls onto the gravel shoulder and brakes. Jason leaps out, slams the door. There is the smell of mesquite and heat, a hot engine, and dust. Jude yanks the pillow from the car and tosses it onto the ground. The foam bits deep inside it are burning, turning black. The yellow case that Rita made is being eaten by the sticky little flames.

She worries about the kid. He's standing alongside the highway, looking like he's going to faint, paler than usual and swaying. He looks like he's going to jump into the fire, to stomp on it in his sandalled feet. She's ready to pull him out, but instead he stalks out into the mesquite. A tumbleweed gets loose and bounces across the highway. The grille of a truck rumbling past gathers it up. Blowing dust, the truck gives her a honk. Bastard, Jude thinks.

She turns to yell at Jason, but he's already back. Noises come from his throat, through jaws and teeth clamped tight. He's crying or laughing, she can't tell which. He won't look straight at her, he won't let her touch him. He takes his teddy bear from the car and walks over to the fire. He drops it in. Next he collects his new pack of colored pencils, his fish books and his Magic Slate and drops each of them into the flames, one by one, even the open bag of Cheetos.

Jude feels like she had when talking to the next governor. Scared to death. The guy was actually praying for Rita. The praying part undid her, loosened her knees. Praying is such an old-fashioned thing, so out-dated, so right-wing. Keeps America safe for democracy. Keeps the Commies at bay. The sort of thing Auntie Alice and Uncle Henry are into in a serious way, twice a day.